First published in Great Britain in 2008 by Comma Press
www.commapress.co.uk

A CIP catalogue record of this book is available from the British Library

ISBN: 1905583230
EAN: 978-1905583232

Supported by The Liverpool Capital of Culture as part of theCities on the Edge
and Liverpool 2008 European Capital of Culture programmes

Project part-funded by the European Union

The City of Liverpool

The publishers also gratefully acknowledge assistance from the Arts Council
England North West.

Set in Bembo by David Eckersall
Printed and bound in England by SRP Ltd, Exeter.

ReBerth

Stories from Cities on the Edge

Edited by
Jim Hinks

Foreword by
Franco Bianchini
& Jude Bloomfield

Acknowledgments

'Everyone Has a Skeleton in the Cupboard' first appeared as 'Jeder hat eine Leiche im Keller' in *Die Milchstraße* copyright © 2002 by Hoffmann und Campe Verlag, Hamburg. Reproduced by permission. 'Midday Mania' first appeared as 'Mittagspausenrausch' in *Bremer Texte 3*, copyright © Edition Temmen, Bremen 2006. Reproduced by permission. 'Silver Rain' first appeared as 'Srebrny Deszcz' in *Pierwsza miłość i inne opowiadania* (Puls, London 1996). Copyright © Paweł Huelle. Reproduced by arrangement with S.I.W. Znak Sp. z o.o., Krakow, Poland. 'Witomińska Street' first appeared as 'Witomińska' in *Sam* (Gdansk University Press, 2006). Copyright © Adam Kamiński. Reproduced by permission of the author. 'The End of the Quays' first appeared as 'Au bout du quai' in *Vivre Fatigue* (J'ai Lu, 1998). Reproduced by arrangement with the publisher and Agence Hoffman. 'The Cave and the Footbridge' first appeared in 'La grotte et la passerelle' in *Un toit, nouvelles sur le logement* (Editions Cherche-Midi, 2006). The novel excerpt reproduced in the story is from Christian Garcin's novel *L'Embankment* (Gallimard, 2003). Both texts © Copyright Christian Garcin 2006. Reproduced by permission of the author. 'Right In the Eyes' first appeared as 'Dritto dritto negli occhi' in *Mosca più balena* (minimum fax, 2003). Copyright © Valeria Parrella. Reproduced by arrangement with the publisher. 'Beneath the Torragaveta Sun' first appeared as 'Sotto il sole di Torre Gaveta', in *Una Vita Postdatata* by Peppe Lanzetta. Copyright © Giangiacomo Feltrinelli Editore Milano. First edition in "Universale Economica Feltrinelli", April 1998. Reproduced by permission. 'The Terminal' first appeared as 'Esenler Otogarı' in *Kadından Kentler* (Metis Publications, 2008). Copyright © Murathan Mungan/Metis Publications. Reproduced by permission. 'Aborted City' first appeared as 'Sehir Düşüğü' in *Siftah* (Varlık Yayınları, 2000). Copyright © Hatice Meryem. Reproduced by permission of the author.

CONTENTS

CONTENTS

Foreword

Cities on the Edge was conceived as an international collaboration between six port cities – Bremen, Gdansk, Istanbul, Liverpool, Marseilles and Naples – and their cultural organisations. It sought to build on common characteristics and problems that port cities face such as the contraction of port activities, gentrification, displacement and dislocation of the working class population and global migration no longer contained or protected within the 'space of mixing' of the immediate port area. Rather than treating these as intractable problems, the project aimed to capitalise on them as strengths – traditions of dissidence, irony, and tension towards national political, economic and cultural establishments – and mobilise their imaginative and intellectual resources.

The Cities on the Edge project – initiated as part of the European dimension of Liverpool Capital of Culture 2008 – puts the artists and intellectuals (including the writers in this collection) in the lead, encouraging them to explore the multiple meanings of 'edge' in the six cities, not only signifying geographical or political marginality but a border and point of exchange between different worlds: for example, Islam-Christianity and Asia-Europe for Istanbul, Europe and North Africa for Marseilles, and Germanic and Slavic cultures in the case of Gdansk (the latter being one of the themes in Paweł Huelle's story in this collection). Other meanings of 'edge' in the six cities are found in the presence of deep-seated poverty, lives that are lived on the social margin, forced to the edge of existence, or lived in the hollows and on the periphery of the urban fabric – as well as 'edginess' in artistic production and cultural life.

The premise of Cities on the Edge is that port cities live on the edge of their nations, in tension with their capitals, drawn outward by the pull of sea, the transitory movement and settlement of migrants on their shores, the need for solidarity and resilience to counter the vicissitudes of employment, weather, and time. The people of these cities are also, historically, driven inward by the solitariness of the sea and the anarchic individualism of seamen's and dockers' lives, a rebellious spirit, quick wit and ironic humour, and fierce local loyalty expressed through allegiance to the city's football teams.

If these were the conscious aspects of the six cities' mindscapes, the stories in this anthology chip away at some of their more romantic and optimistic political connotations. In this collection, we find distinctive voices worn away by the incessant tides of change, defeat, and marginalisation, rather than rebellion or resistance. Where the voices are hopeful, they are steeped in fantasy like the two friends, in Bremen in Artur Becker's story, videoing their own lives and going on dope trips to Amsterdam, or, also in Bremen, the married woman, in Claudia Parman's story, escaping to the Weser waterfront to recall her lost lover during her lunch breaks.

The title of this collection, *ReBerth,* implies a rebirth of port cities, and yet these short stories pose a question mark over such a renewal. Rather, they suggest that if these cities are to live again, they will not do so primarily as ports. In all six cities, former docks have been or are being transformed into marinas, expensive flats, up-market shops, hotels, bars and public spaces which look the same the world over. Gérard, the central character in Jean-Claude Izzo's story, expresses his fear that Marseilles will lose its distinctiveness and become a playground for the rich, when he says 'One day you'll wake up and find it's not your place any more. It'll be like Nice, only bigger, and even more stupid!'

These cities have lost substantial parts of their port functions, which had spawned distinctive literary and cinematic representations, and it is more difficult than in the past to identify a Gestalt, a metaphor of the city as a whole. Yet these stories convey a very distinctive sense of place. They are studded with motifs that embody some aspect of local society – deindustrialisation, social isolation and exclusion, the negative sides of modernity – such as the rubbish in Istanbul and Naples in 'Aborted City' and 'Beneath the Torregaveta Sun' respectively. In the Torregaveta story, the 'seaside Bronx' of Naples is black with sewage and tar, and the beach encrusted with detritus. The place is literally the opposite of 'sanitised' upmarket resorts like the Seychelles, the Maldives or nearby Capri. And yet Torregaveta has a plebeian vitality and humanity, made of 'music cassettes… onion frittatas, egg frittatas, aubergines, cockles… stories of love and squalor.'

Extreme social polarisation appears in several stories, including 'Aborted City' by Hatice Meryem, in which the well-heeled residents of Istanbul live in 'gated communities' overlooking the alleys and doorways inhabited by street children, and Alexei Sayle's 'Bread, Circuses and Replica Shirts', where a young Spanish Liverpool FC footballer is shocked and intrigued by the boarded up houses and other signs of urban dereliction surrounding Anfield Stadium, the home of one of the world's most iconic and financially mighty football brands. Indeed in all six cities economic inequality is visible, in the contrast between regenerated parts of city centres (offering a myriad of opportunities for tourists and well-off residents) and inner city or peripheral areas suffering from multiple deprivation.

Because of their histories as ports, all six cities have important traditions of multi-ethnicity and cosmopolitanism, which have continued in recent years, with the concentration of legal and undocumented immigrants in neighbourhoods like Belsunce in Marseilles, Ferrovia in Naples and Osterholz-Tenever in Bremen. In the case of Istanbul, the eponymous reflectedterminal of Murathan Mungan's story acts as a metaphor for the Turkish megalopolis in its chaotic modernisation – a container of people of all backgrounds, ages and nationalities passing through from town to countryside, province to metropolis, known to unknown.

Other images in these stories offer a perspective on the city from the viewpoint of immigrants and outsiders, who often live in the more deprived and marginal areas, such as the hermit in the no man's land near the old port in Marseilles in Christian Garcin's geography. These are places of anonymity and chance, decay and arbitrariness of fate. Only Polish migrant Tadek Brozio and his German friend Koko, in Becker's 'Everyone has a Skeleton in the Cupboard', who do not feel rooted in Bremen, choose where they want to live – in a tower block which takes them imaginatively beyond the confines of the city, giving a wider view of the world. In the Liverpudlian tale 'Scent', by Dinesh Allirajah, even though the river Mersey 'washes the whole city', the endless repetition of the tide acts as a counterpoint to the arbitrariness of events in the rest of the story. In this story, the tide no longer regulates fate: the power of the sea is subjugated.

The imaginary urban landscape of these port cities has become more fragmented, and this is reflected in the rich social characterisation of these stories, which offer a diverse range of perspectives. Valeria Parrella's 'Right in the Eyes', a sustained first person monologue of the Naples' female sub-proletariat gets inside the head of the *Guapetella* who trades on her beauty, plotting her social advance through strategic economic moves while remaining entirely dependent – both sexually and economically – on the local mafia (the *camorra*) and combining generosity and cruelty, typical of her circumscribed choices. In a context of deindustrialisation and declining employment opportunities (in Naples as well as in many other port cities), dependency on organised crime can be the only viable social ladder for the aspirant working class. The internal monologue of the redundant docker in Izzo's 'The End of the Quays' also enables us to enter an inner world of resentment, defeat and resignation that has overwhelmed many workers displaced by containerisation and the contraction of the port. Many other socially marginalised figures populate the stories – but they are invoked from different standpoints: as a threatening, malignant presence in 'Scent', in which a tattoo-daubed, menacing underclass figure, with Doberman dog and studded leather apparel, smashes his girlfriend's furniture and face; from the outside but empathetically as barefoot street children in the Istanbul story 'Aborted City'; as phantom projections of the narrator in Garcin's Marseilles.

Significantly, the characters in these stories tend towards personal, internalised acts of dissent or subjugation, exclusive of an organised political framework: the rebel contestation has been replaced by resignation or adaptation to brutal realities – the docker drawn to an inexorable logic in Izzo's Marseilles, the street children who sarcastically propose neutering rather than giving birth in Hatice Meryem's Istanbul. In cities historically renowned for the accomplishments of a male labour force (of dockers and seafarers), the female protagonists in these stories often adopt private forms of resistance, evidenced by the *Guapetella's* duplicity, and the defiance of the narrator in 'Aborted City' who after miscarrying 'wrote the bastard's name on a cigarette and inhaled it slowly.'

Literature and film enable us to read the emotions of the city that colour the urban imaginary, manifest here in the lyrical tone of the writing, not least in the Polish stories – 'Witomińska Street' by Adam Kamiński and 'Silver Rain' by Paweł Huelle. These Gdansk stories are steeped in the city's tragic history of loss, displacement and nostalgia coming back to haunt the survivors, following the expulsion of the remaining German residents at the end of the Second World War and their replacement with ethnic Poles, many of whom had been deported by the Soviet Union after its annexation of the eastern part of pre-war Poland. The kingdom of death hovers on the edge of Adam Kamiński's 'Witomińska Street', where cars crash into chestnut trees and hearses carry the dead to the cemetery. For Kamiński's young narrator, life collides with dream, fear and fantasy become entwined, and a childhood memory is suddenly disrupted by a surreal moment of horror. 'Silver Rain's darkly comic fairytale form is a modern parable of the dangers of trying to profit from the misery of the past.

The sense of anxiety and sadness which pervades this anthology is leavened by a desperate irony. Moments of happiness turn out to be illusory or short-lived, a mindset perhaps best exemplified by the elderly lady in 'The Terminal', who warns Zozan to adapt her expectations accordingly. But these stories offer hope of a different kind. By understanding our cities' problems – by giving voice to the disenfranchised, the overlooked, the submerged, and acknowledging that this very 'edginess' forges cultural productivity – we take the first tentative steps towards renewal; to building an alternative urban landscape that turns the Cities on the Edge into cutting edge cities once more.

Franco Bianchini and Jude Bloomfield
Liverpool, Nov 08

Introduction

Liverpool is built on stories. There are conflicting stories about its origins as a settlement, for example, and the etymology of its name. There are stories of how it grew, of the dubious ways it made its fortune; stories charting its recessions and renaissances, its struggles and triumphs. Some are celebratory stories, while others we might prefer to forget. These stories are part of the myth of Liverpool and fundamental to its identity.

Besides these shared, civic stories, everyone has their own story of Liverpool, their own personal version of the city, forged from their interactions with it. The tourist who visits the Albert Dock, the Tate and the Cavern Club – the officially sanctioned narrative of the city – conceives a very different Liverpool to the teenager in the backstreets of Toxteth or Kensington. The Liverpool inhabited by a small child is different to the Liverpool of an older person, inevitably overlaid with the topography of memory. There isn't one Liverpool, just as there's no single Bremen or Gdansk, nor one Istanbul or Naples or Marseilles. Each of these cities is a mosaic of stories and perspectives, in constant flux, being constantly rewritten.

ReBerth collects short stories from each of the 'Cities on the Edge' – with two new stories set in Liverpool, by Alexei Sayle and Dinesh Allirajah, and specially commissioned translations of stories from Bremen, Gdansk, Istanbul, Marseilles and Naples. It doesn't claim to offer a definitive picture of Liverpool (or any of the other Cities on the Edge), because there isn't one Liverpool. Nor does it pretend to furnish the reader with a truly representative sample of the contemporary short fiction from these cities. However, with the recommendations of translators and literature professionals on the ground in each city, we've arrived at a selection that engages with some of the challenges the Cities on the Edge have recently faced; a selection in which their rapidly changing economic, cultural and architectural vistas might be glimpsed momentarily, refracted through the prism of short fiction.

ReBerth is in fact the latest in a series of Comma Press anthologies featuring short stories from cities in Europe and the Middle East. It's our view that short stories, in particular, commend themselves to translation and intercultural dialogue: their brevity often inclines them to transposable situations and characters (if not universal ones), in comparison to the multi-layered novel, while they're largely unencumbered by rhyme and meter, which might cling more tenaciously to the specifics of a language. Moreover, the short form is particularly adept at exploring the dynamic between narrative and the urban environment. Short stories have a long tradition of depicting encounters between strangers. This intermixing invariably happens in municipal public space; indeed, the peculiarities of these spaces frequently inform the narrative mechanism of a story. The stories in *ReBerth* are a case in point. Throughout this anthology, the city is a tangible presence – almost a character in its own right – interceding in the lives of its inhabitants; its streets and alleyways ushering them towards confrontation or reunion, its quays and rivers leading them towards adventure or epiphany.

Sequentially, these stories take us on a round-trip. From Liverpool, we'll steam briskly south, and then up the English Channel to Bremen (by way of the River Weser). After that we'll round the horn of Denmark and sail into the Baltic to visit the neighbouring ports of Gdansk and Gdynia. Next we set a long course back round the Iberian peninsular and into the Med, visiting Marseilles, Naples and eventually Istanbul, before arriving safely back on the Liverpool quayside. But be warned: there will be no cabaret, and the quoits and deckchairs will remain stowed below deck. We'll be avoiding the clamour and crush of the usual beauty spots. The cities in *ReBerth* are not the versions depicted in Tourist Information brochures, but cities as experienced by a cohort of marginalised and sometimes unsavoury characters.

In many cases these authors are writing directly against the officially sanctioned, sanitised version of their city's story. Instead they give voice to those residing in dimly-lit backstreets - which appear ever darker next to the glare of urban regeneration projects - or beside neglected, rubbish-strewn beaches, across the water from pristine holiday resorts. If anything might be said to characterise the literature of the Cities on the Edge, it's perhaps this urge to document social and economic disparity; indeed, a palpable spirit of dissent runs through many of the stories in *ReBerth*, by writers who won't shut up and behave themselves, normalise or neuter the city in the face of global economic forces.

While unified in their candour, these stories encompass a broad range of literary styles. Some authors, such as Paweł Huelle, Adam Kamiński and Claudia Parman, epitomise the European short story tradition, fusing delicate characterisation with lyrical depictions of a landscape. Others - perhaps unsurprisingly in a collection of European port city stories - embrace transatlantic influences, as evidenced by Murathan Mungan's Altmanesque journey through the secret thoughts, regrets and aspirations of people passing through Istanbul's busy Esenler bus terminal, or Artur Becker's story of economic migrants slumming around in marijuana-clouded apartments, dreaming of making it rich. Two stories here attempt to wriggle free from the traditional classification of what a short story is, borrowing heavily from other forms: Peppe Lanzetta weaves a conventional narrative through a kind of visceral, instinctive prose poetry, in response to the squalor of Naples' Torregaveta Beach, while in Christian Garcin's 'The Cave and the Footbridge' the author fuses autobiography and fiction to meditate on the process of writing Marseilles and its people.

The Cities on the Edge may have finally turned the page on the days of a maritime economy and embraced new economic models, but it's their people who will shape their future, not their shopping malls or quayside apartments. Alongside the official narratives of regeneration and tourism, there are a plethora of alternative, personal stories being written each day; myriad new versions of these cities taking form. As long as a loud cacophony of voices – including those of the writers in this anthology – is permitted to ring out, it's to be hoped that homogenisation can be obviated, and that these cities can remain edgy, regardless of the economic model they adopt. As such, the disparate and often difficult voices in this anthology don't represent the death throes of cities on the wane, but the birthing pains of cities deciding what the will become next.

Jim Hinks
Liverpool, Nov 08

LIVERPOOL

Scent

DINESH ALLIRAJAH

The fight in the flat across the hallway announces itself with a demure fanfare. If he were to close a book he'd finished reading, and declare it closed with an emphatic smack of the cover, the sound would match the hollow thud just heard. The silence that follows the thud hangs like a breath held but on the point of being let go. And then his walls begin to quiver, shouts and screams collide, and the howls of his neighbours' two dogs stretch out into one constant siren.

He is sitting upright at the end of his bed. He has only his bed for a seat. It is the one purchase he has made in the two weeks since he signed the lease for his Housing Association flat, and then re-read the agreement to find the clause he'd overlooked about it being unfurnished. The flat has a bare hardboard floor worn to a stiff sponge. The interior walls seem barely thicker than a film of wallpaper paste, within which hundreds of tiny wood chips are embedded. It all forms a fragile shell that now encases the sounds of fighting.

The noise cloaks him and he slumps forward to bury his face in his hands. The scent from his fingertips dashes against his eyes and nose like a slingshot of small pebbles. The flavours take turns to make their mark – lemongrass, wet soil, petrol, jasmine – and he remains on his bed, held by the smell, until it's time to leave for work.

★

The days follow a tidal pattern, out from the flat, into work, out again, and back into the flat. If he were to step outside the pattern, the ground under his feet would wash away like sand under an incoming wave. He keeps to a pattern in work as well, while the River Mersey waits beneath him. He arranges his bottles – taller ones at the side, smaller in the middle; clear glass at the front, colours and metal at the back – a team photograph of grinning nozzles.

His responsibilities revolve around the bottles. When he's finished arranging them, he organises the cotton wool buds across a folded napkin on an egg-shaped dish. He folds the black flannels which match his shirt and trousers, and places them in front of the bottles, alongside the dish, on the fold-out table the other side of the hand-dryer from the urinals. He crouches down to fetch combs and a half-pint glass from his crate of supplies underneath the table. He loses balance momentarily and a knee touches the floor, but he's able to steady himself on the table and return to his feet. A glance at his trouser-leg confirms no mess or moisture and he adds the combs to his display. The bar has just opened for the night. Everything in the gent's toilet is clean and polished. The walls are able to display their silken indigo colour, like the water in a midnight harbour lit by incoming ships. The aluminium sheen of the troughs is unbroken by tidemarks or droplets of spit. And the soles of his feet hover above the river that washes the whole city.

Most men do not see him when they enter. They go to the urinal, stiff-backed or slouched according to the time of night. It's only when they turn to the sink that they see him and this is when he speaks. 'Scent?'

It is the only word he's required to speak in his job. After the first few times, he stops noticing it as it comes out of his mouth. It becomes a spray that hangs in the air. The men are polite as they walk past the table. Most will meet his eyes with a brief glance, and then walk past with a contrite bow of the head. He imagines that inspiring this mixture of self-consciousness and guilt must be what it feels like to be a nun.

Those who stop to hover over the bottles never ask his advice as to which scent they should wear. He would recommend that they find the one they came out with, not attempt to mask the new smells they've acquired from the drinks and the smokers' doorways, with something even more pungent. He would suggest that these layers build to give them a fragrance that stiffens the air they move through. He worries about what it does to the water; wonders what a squirt of Hugo Boss will do to the ancient mating rituals of the eels that find their ways into the estuary. The men, when they speak to him, call him 'mate'; they call him 'lad'. Two or more of them visiting the toilet together will stand either side of him to continue their conversations, like neighbours on adjoining balconies.

'Awww – whassat yer puttin' on?'

'Quick splash of the auld Gucci – cheers lad. Don't wanna hit the titty bars without freshening up first.'

'Tony, they'll have yer *doing* the fuckin' pole dance wearing tha' – smell like a fuckin' tart's knicker drawer there!'

'Yeh, maybe *your* tart's fuckin' knicker drawer, y'knob – all the fuckin' visitors *she's* 'ad – nice one, mate. Here you go.'

Fifty pence drops into the half-pint glass. The Gucci bottle is wiped and returned to its position in the line-up.

★

Since he moved into his ground-floor flat, there haven't been very many days when the weather outside would justify opening either of the two towering sash windows in his bedroom. He has to climb onto the windowsill of one to get to eye-level with the catch holding the two panes together. When he releases the catch, the lower pane requires a hefty shove upwards to get it to move. It feels like he's been thrown a packed suitcase to catch, and he only manages to open the window a couple of inches.

He has no curtains for his windows yet, just as there is no furniture to accompany his bed. There isn't a curtain long enough to reach all the way down from the top sash; perhaps a ship's sail might. Light washes into the flat all day, and he relies on the night sky for darkness when he's in bed, though this is frequently broken by a security spotlight in the overlooking tower block which, when triggered, drenches his face with light like an interrogator's lamp.

As he climbs down from the window, he sees his neighbour turning into the driveway of their block of flats. It's the first time he has seen him since the loudest fight yet, three nights ago. The neighbour's name is Danny, which he knows from hearing it shouted during previous fights. A new city is strange for dozens of reasons but he has come to recognise that Danny is bizarre, regardless of his address.

Before he sees Danny, he sees his two black Doberman dogs. They scamper around the corner, stumbling as they strain against their taut leads, at once vicious and comical. A second later, Danny appears, holding the two leads with rigid, sleeveless, tattooed arms and standing with equally stiff legs on a skateboard, the pose of an Ancient Roman chariot racer. Head to steel toe-cap, Danny dresses in aggression. The bleached blond spikes in his hair and metal ones around his belt and wrist bands tell of a style evolved through hand-to-hand combat. When his wheels come into contact with the gravel on the drive, Danny leaps down from the skateboard. The momentum of the ride and the continued pull from the dogs has him staggering forward but two shouts and two fierce tugs on their leads have the animals regrouping round their master. When he bends to retrieve the skateboard, they follow his movement and one of the dogs leaps to catch hold of the board in its teeth. Danny shouts at it to let go, wrenching the board so the dog's legs swing away from the ground. It flails but clings on. Danny draws back his right leg. It looks for a moment as if he might kick the dog but instead he brings his knee up, high and hard into the dog's ribs so it falls back onto the gravel, jaws now clamping down on fresh air. Danny tucks the board under his arm and, with both dogs now cowed into an even trot behind him, disappears from view. He reappears, in audio only, with a slam of the front door and more cajoling words as he and the dogs stamp and scrabble into their flat.

The spectacle having ended, he resumes his seat on the end of his bed but, immediately, his doorbell rings. He has not heard its slow double-chime before. The front door's entry phone buzzer has been pressed since he moved in, when his bed was delivered, but the doorbell is only for people already in the building. He looks through the spyhole and sees only bleached blond spikes, which then fall back to be replaced by a magnified eyeball, staring back at him.

Disembarked from his skateboard, Danny is taller than him only by virtue of his motorcycle boots and the vertical hairstyle. Nonetheless, he has a voice and array of gestures to overwhelm whichever space he's in.

'I need to get shot of me furniture.' A finger stabs each word as he says it. 'You need some furniture – jus' moved in, yeh? Bed, nothin' else. You wanna get some curtains up an' all. D'you wan' this furniture or wha'?'

He hesitates, but Danny has already bustled past him, inside to the expanse of bare hardboard surrounding the bed.

'Tell you wha' – I got all this stuff, couple of cupboards, sofa, table. If you wan' it – fifty quid, the lot.'

It's barely half what he paid for the bed. He asks Danny if he's sure about the price.

'Deffo, yeah – I just need shot of it. It's me girlfriend's flat – ex, like – she's away for a couple of days and then she's kicking me out. Come 'ead – have a look what there is.'

Danny leads him across the hallway and they are in the flat with the two suspicious but exhausted Dobermans. Unlike in his studio flat, comprising just a bedroom and kitchen, the bedroom in Danny's flat is separate from the room in which they are now standing. The focal point appears to be a circle of scatter cushions, ashtrays, dog bowls and a television with a blackened screen. Everything else is pushed to the walls. He has no time to observe more because he has to follow Danny through each doorway in the flat two or three times, with nothing accomplished except a brief argument with the dogs. The conversation sweeps him up and he has to accept each direction it takes. Danny says he's just going 'to do one.' The cash will be enough to get him out of town. Danny instructs him to help tip the contents of a dresser onto the floor. He worries about smashing a pile of plates on the bottom of three shelves above a cupboard with two sliding doors but, as he removes the top two plates, he sees that each is already split in two; a broken clock and smashed photo frame are also swept off the shelves. When the dresser is empty, he takes hold of one end to carry it across to his own flat where they position it against the wall next to his bed.

Twenty minutes later, there is a wooden picnic table with two bench seats in the kitchen, a bureau with a fold-out desk that matches the dresser, a chair for the desk, and a small wardrobe. There is a pile of cushions on the floor, stripped from a sofa that has until now been an incongruous presence in Danny's kitchen because it was too large for any other room. There are three firm seat cushions, and a cluster of slightly smaller, plumper cushions to provide back and side support, but the sofa's immense base is unable to negotiate the space between the flat door and the bedroom. Danny has been lifting and carrying in perpetual motion but this dilemma has brought him to a halt. He looks up at the window facing the front driveway.

'Can you get that open?' He doesn't wait for a reply but jumps onto the windowsill and pushes at the lower sash. 'Jammed,' he murmurs as he jumps down, and jogs back to his flat. When he reappears he has a hammer in his hand that looks as though it has been held there since birth. Back on the windowsill, he issues three sharp taps that rattle the flat and set the dogs barking. Then, with a sudden upward swing of an arm, like a boxer administering an uppercut, he throws the window open.

Still holding the hammer, Danny jumps down again. 'Wait there. You can 'ave this an' all, la, might come in handy.' He hands over the hammer and disappears.

It's a heavy tool, the handle covered in tightly-wound white gaffer tape to facilitate a firmer grip. The feel of the hammer pulls him away from the sensation of swimming amongst his new furniture and he thinks about the banging and screaming from Danny's flat the other night. He thinks about the absent girlfriend and the hasty escape from the city.

'Grab hold!' calls a voice from outside his window.

He looks up to see the base of a sofa leaning through the wide open window. Its nylon covering has a dramatic pattern of broad diagonal, muted gold and murky brown stripes that match the cushions piled up on his floor. He holds onto the end of the sofa and is slowly pushed back until most of it is inside.

Danny returns to help carry the base into position, then arranges the cushions in one last muscular frenzy before accepting the £50, in four tens and the past fortnight's tips, and leaving.

He sits upright on the edge of the sofa. The hammer sits on the end of the bed. He looks around at new shadows, interruptions to the stretch of featureless hardboard on the floor and wood-chip on the walls, and he leans back until his head finds a head-shaped well in one of the cushions.

★

The evening arrives at the Albert Dock complex in gradual flecks and clusters of darkness, crowding out the daylight.

Anyone walking between the shops and restaurants, outspanning the largest of the docks, are either preparing to go home or arriving to work; there is no pressing business. Nobody seems fully to belong but nor does anyone intrude. He finds a place to watch the water and gulp down the last clean air he'll taste before his shift.

In the water below the Tate Gallery, he sees an eel insinuating its way around the dock walls. Two jellyfish bob to the surface. He recognises their bleakly luminous purple colouring and mutters, 'Pelagia noctiluna.'

'There's another, Dad! And another! *And* another! There's hundreds of jellyfish in Liverpool!'

A young boy has appeared beside him, leaning on the railings with his father to peer into the water. As he looks and talks, the boy flaps his arms in languid figures of eight to resemble the movements of the jellyfish.

'How cool is that?' says the dad. 'How many can you count?'

The boy locks into an intense scrutiny of the dock waters. 'There… are… at least… thir-ty thousand and fifty hundred.'

'Wow!' says the dad. 'That's a huge… er, school. School. Shoal? Not quite sure what the name is for a big bunch of jellyfish.'

'Is it – a bunch?'

'No, but – never mind.'

'Is it a herd, Dad?'

'No, that's cows, mate. They don't swim that well.'

'Excuse me.' He edges towards the two strangers. 'Sorry, I could hear – it's called a smack. A jellyfish group is a smack of jellyfish.'

They stare back at him for a few seconds before the dad grins. 'Cheers, mate. Nice one.' He tousles the boy's hair. 'Now you know, eh, son – it's a smack. Not like the ones your sister gives you.'

The boy continues to stare, then launches into his

jellyfish mime. 'This is how a jellyfish swims.'

He laughs and copies the mime, to the boy's delight. 'Ah, but you should know they are actually not swimming. Jellyfish only drift on the current. They don't decide "Where should we go?" And this –' he repeats the mime and notices that he's wafting a medley of aftershave fragrance towards the boy and his father. 'This is to attract prey. It makes tiny sea creatures believe they're swimming with the current but instead they are being drawn towards the jellies.' His accurate replication of the jellyfish's pulsations becomes a far cruder mime of something gobbling a mouthful of food.

It's time for work. He leaves his audience; the dad winks and the boy waves. He walks around the dock to where the only word he'll need to say is 'Scent.'

*

One drawback of having furniture is that he now has a multitude of places in or on which to leave his door keys, which in turn increases his chances of forgetting them when he leaves the flat. The flat door, which he has just shut behind him, has a Yale lock and a mortise, so the moment he realises he's unable to double lock the door, he also knows he's locked himself out.

There's a gust of panic. He stands, clinging to the door frame, and considers kicking down the door. He pictures aiming a high kick in the area of the Yale lock. The fantasy intensifies with each replay, until the moment the door splinters open and the impact is accompanied by a shotgun blast. He steps back from the door. He'll have time to call into the Housing Association office before work.

The front door of the building opens and he is joined in the communal hallway by a young woman. In her smart blue skirt and jacket, with dyed red hair pulled back into a ponytail, it takes a few moments for him to recognise her as Danny's former girlfriend from the opposite ground floor flat. She gives him a tight smile and hurries past but she slows when she notices him standing, facing his flat, not moving.

'Are you OK?'

She walks over and places a hand on his right arm. It's a momentary, simple action to get his attention but he's startled by the warmth that clings to his shirt when her hand moves away.

'Thank you, yes, I've – I'm just locked out of my flat.'

'Oh no!' She bites her bottom lip and shudders, as though from a sudden sharp pain. 'D'you need a hand to get back in?'

He looks at the concern on her face and sees also a reddening around her left cheekbone, that's a duller red than her lipstick or her hair. He shakes his head. 'It's no problem. Thank you.'

'OK, but – I'm just across the hall if you need help.'

'I know,' he smiles. 'It's good to meet you.' He offers his hand and her face wrinkles into puzzled amusement as she shakes it.

He walks towards the front door. Looking over his shoulder, he can see his neighbour. She's now the one standing still in the middle of the hallway. She sniffs the fingertips of her right hand, and he can see a soft, private smile starting to take shape.

BREMEN

Midday Mania

CLAUDIA PARMAN

'Do you like living in Bremen?'

I don't know what made me ask the question. It was addressed to the lawyer who looked after our firm's constitutional affairs. I knew her in no other capacity than this, but I liked working with her, for she was a calm, cultured person with remarkable charisma. She was about ten years my senior, and every time I saw her I wished I could be like her. She seemed distinguished, always carried herself well, and always got straight down to business, without being impersonal. She was well turned out, though not ostentatiously so, a style I had yet to acquire. Her makeup was light, her skin was velvety and a little transparent. She wore her slightly thin, light brown hair loosely gathered at the back of her head.

She looked at me calmly and impassively with her pretty, clever, grey-green eyes as my question passed between us. Suddenly she appeared very sad and introspective. Then it was as if, right in front of my eyes, she opened up a door into her psyche. She started to speak, and all at once her voice was quite changed, strangely monotone. She told me, laconically:

'I feel very attached to Bremen. But my attachment goes far beyond what you probably understand by the term. This city is like a drug for me – an ersatz drug.'

She paused at this point, straightening her shoulders a little and shaping a fresh tension back into her body. 'A little while ago, I used to meet up with a man. We weren't having a relationship as such, we just liked one another. He was a teacher with reduced hours, so he had quite a bit of free time. He often used to wait for me around midday, and we would walk along the Schlachte promenade together. We liked it best down there by the water. It was lovely. Suddenly I felt alive in a way I had long forgotten. I was very happy when I saw him. I didn't notice straight away that this happiness was so addictive.

'It only became clear to me when, one day, he wasn't there. Then I started to do my walks without him. Every day I would manage to keep the thinking part of me functioning until midday. Some time ago I realised that thought processes can simply be reduced to a series of mechanical actions. And since then, this is how I've functioned: my work, my thinking, is just little cogs rotating, and each cog turns the next. I make it through to midday like this. Every day, at about 12:30, I avoid any colleagues who might want to have lunch with me. First of all, I look after my physical needs; if it's cloudy or wet I go to the Karstądt department store and eat a salad, then I walk a little way along the River Weser. I have to see the water, every day.

'On overcast days, there's no danger of my mania setting in. The cloudy weather has my best interests at heart, for then the water is a dull, leaden brew and I don't need to bother looking for a certain colour in it, a grey-blue that I love more than anything else. Hiding away, the sun leaves my soul in peace; maybe there's a stiff breeze that chafes at the skin on my face, or maybe it's even raining. No loving couples are walking along the promenade, and I have no hope of finding that person who is so special to me leisurely strolling along. On particularly good days there is both wind and rain, and I can't even open an umbrella. Then my face gets a sharp shower and I wake up quickly, well before my dreams can start to take hold of me. I go back to the office, and my hair and makeup are ruined, but my inner life is still intact. My chores quickly take the upper hand and, still able to concentrate on my work, I can go home early and spend the evening with my husband.

'But the bad days come when the sun shines. Then an invisible fishing line draws me directly down to the water. The narrow Böttcher Street passage makes my head start to spin. I literally feel endorphins sluicing around my brain as I walk past the little street's pretty window displays. When I take the tunnel down to the Weser on Martini Street, it's like passing into another sphere. By the time I come back into daylight at the side of the river, those mechanical rules that control my conscious actions have all been broken. It's as if someone has thrown a little stick into the cogs of my brain. At the Weser I give myself over entirely to my emotions. My actions and my thoughts become completely impulsive. My eyes look for familiar markers, and my body reacts directly to what they see. Each place I recognise stimulates me, making my insides churn. I look at the blue-grey Weser – and am looking into his eyes; I feel a gentle tickle in my stomach. The wind brushes lightly over my shoulders – every breath is like his embrace; my heart begins to thump loudly. I lean back against the sandstone wall that has been warmed by the sun – and feel the pleasing temperature of his smooth skin; my body loosens up. The windows along Teerhof island behold a pair of lovers. The ships docked at the Martini quay melt away into the thought of travelling with him to distant lands. I walk along the river and touch, see, smell one memory after another. I am intoxicated with happiness. I stay standing a little while longer in front of the tunnel under Tiefer Street, playing for time before I cross back over to the other side. For a moment, I have this little glimmer of hope in me. I look into every face, scrutinise distant figures as well. I know that going into the tunnel means entering into darkness. Then I am moving through the gloomy shaft of a deep well. But this is just the come-down after my high. The Schnoor Quarter is a blur as I walk through it. Quickly across the market place, and I'm back in my office. These afternoons are wasted, as far as my work's concerned. The secretary's worried looks are enough of a mirror for me. 'What exhausting weather,' she says then, full of sympathy. She brings me a pot of boiling water to make myself a herbal tea. She closes my office door behind her, taking the folder of papers I should have signed with her. I hold the cup that he once gave me, the calming tea cradled in my hand. I rummage around in my treasure chest, my private drawer, and fetch out a stone. It is grey, encircled by two white lines which cross over on the front and back. It lies coolly in my hand, but it was warm when he found it for me. I try to restore this warmth to the stone, but my hands, in spite of the sun, are cold as death. I touch the envelope holding his letters in my drawer and decide which letter I will read as evening approaches – as a reward, if I do manage to do some work after all. Then I take out a little mirror, touch up my mascara, and, very slowly and carefully, I find my way back into my mechanical world.

'On days like these, I stay late. When my colleagues have gone I read a letter, wait a little while for a call that doesn't come, play around with my mobile, draft and reject sentences in my head. When I finally do get home, my husband will ask me kindly: a hard day at work today? And I will answer him: yes, I just had to get something finished before I left. Then we sit down opposite one another and eat. He tells me about his day, and I smile.'

She glanced at her watch, it was already midday. I was completely stunned by her tale. She offered me her arm, smiling. 'Come on,' she said cheerfully, her eyes shining. 'It's such lovely weather. Let's take a walk along the Weser!'

Translated from the German by Rebecca Braun

Everyone has a Skeleton in the Cupboard

ARTUR BECKER

1.

Coins never smiled up at me from the pavement. I'm serious. I wasn't even able to find ten pfennigs, which was causing me considerable concern, because I'd promised my friends in Poland that one day I'd come back with a briefcase full of deutschmarks and make all their dreams come true. 'Tickets for the Pink Floyd concert in Hamburg – no problem!' I had said back then. 'A four week sailing holiday on the Śniardwy and Mamry Lakes – couldn't be easier, guys!'

Sixteen years had passed since my generous promise and I was still unable to fulfil it, but I was working on it, or, more to the point: I, Tadek Brozio, was literally working my ass off to get stinking rich.

I even bought myself a Japanese pedometer, one that attached itself to your foot with a velcro strap. Working in a warehouse, I covered huge distances every day, like an Ethiopian marathon runner. My record up to now – twenty-eight kilometres – in ten hours. Not that anyone believed me, not even Koko, my German friend, the guy I lived with.

We shared a small flat on the tenth floor of a concrete apartment block development in Bremen. When we decided to move in together, Koko said it absolutely had to be a high-rise building, because then you had a view that would finally

17

open your eyes and show you how big the world really is.

Koko was passionate about taking the lift. He loved science fiction films above all else, and in a lift he felt like an astronaut being raised up the launching pad to the space capsule. The ideas he sometimes had!

Incidentally, Koko was the only German who, in my book, could have been a Russian, because he had a big heart, wasn't afraid of anything, and because only in the icy North was he able to keep his blood pressure halfway stable. He needed the cold like the air he breathed — in the sun he immediately turned feverish and got sick. It was for exactly this reason that he took his leave of Freiburg ten years ago and came to Bremen, even though he would rather have emigrated to Murmansk.

My friend even spoke Russian. He didn't learn it at university, nor did he idolize Trotsky or Prince Myschkin. No, Koko was after the country's women — and how many times had he travelled to Russia just for that! His longest stay was on a farm belonging to a certain Sawickij near to Nischnij Nowgorod. Ten months in total. Since then he spoke better Russian than I did. His nickname even came from there. *Koko* was what this Sawickij used to call his home-brewed schnapps. My friend was always able to keep up well when they drank, and at some point this farmer said to him, 'You are a germanskij *Koko!*'

In 1988 (I was twenty then) I fled the Communists and service in the People's Army and came to West Germany. The fact that I later moved in with, so to speak, a Soviet, and into a concrete high-rise development at that, didn't bother me in the slightest.

Koko and I got along swimmingly. I could stub out my cigarette on the plate I'd just eaten from. Koko didn't complain about my table manners. And I could give free reign to my Polish talent for improvisation. If we were both a bit short, I had no problem living like an asparagus harvester for a month: noodles with tinned goulash for two ninety-nine was fine by me. And when our rent was due and Koko's job helping out in the care home had yet again been cut thanks to new budget measures and there was only a hundred note left in my wallet, then I sometimes went to the Bremen casino and played roulette.

OK, so mostly I lost the last of our money, especially when Koko was with me. He always brought me bad luck: 'Bet on a different one!' was his standard line, then I would stupidly follow his advice and move my counters at the last second, even though I already sensed that we were going to lose again.

'They're all just small fry here, these Hanseatic redheads,' Koko would whisper to me then. 'We'll soon cut them down to size.'

2.

We were bored in the winter, and so one of those sad weekends was coming round again when Koko and I would drive to Amsterdam to get something new to smoke: just two or three little packets with a bit of grass or Afghan Black to cheer us up with a couple of cans in front of the telly. I usually had the early shift on Fridays, and managed to finish up by one, like today.

I was in fine spirits as I climbed into my twelve year old Tadek-Brozio-Mercedes and drove home. I had an S-class, after all, one of the good old ones with chrome bumpers.

I was hardly a saint, but every time I saw the warehouses of our shipping company disappearing in my rear-view mirror, I immediately felt that I was a good person: I was making sure the German state got its taxes, and as long as I carried on running around the place with my pedometer strapped to my foot and loading the boxes of muesli bars and cat food onto the lorries, they would leave me in peace.

For I had brought a terrible affliction over with me from

Poland: fear of a state that was forever interfering in everything, right from birth. So it was particularly important to me not to run the slightest risk of endangering German order, because the Capitalists too liked sniffing around in other people's business, and my greatest enemy was the Job Centre, which was actually remarkably similar to the State Security Service. And how they made you pay for being unemployed! My head hurt just thinking about it.

I parked in front of our apartment block and put the steering lock on, so that our neighbours, the Turks and the Russians, didn't get any bright ideas about taking a little trip in my car – a quickie to Istanbul or Moscow and back again.

Koko was already back, his wheels were parked, as ever, on a double yellow line. He lived for fines, and for his Canon video camera that was always breaking on him. When he took this professional piece of equipment – he'd forked out eight thousand marks for it – out onto the street and began filming, people thought a TV crew was about. Even in Amsterdam, where I have yet to meet a normal person, everyone turned round to stare at us, except for a naked man on roller skates with a Walkman in his hand.

Koko was working on his magnum opus, 'My Life'. He filmed everything he could get his lens on. Not a day went by without him shooting something. His archive of cassettes had meanwhile grown so large that he was gradually losing the overview. But he was always happy: 'There really must be something pretty major going on here. Just look! Fifteen shoeboxes full of video tapes with Koko and Tadek Brozio playing the lead roles. We'll get an Oscar soon and be immortal!'

I took the lift to the tenth floor, marched to our door and opened it. Koko was sitting in the kitchen, poking his little finger in his left ear and slurping an espresso.

His video camera was on a tripod, filming the new scene. 'Koko drinking coffee at the end of a day's work. Friday,

13 February, 1998.'

'Hello,' I said, 'What's up?'

'Hello Tadek,' said Koko. 'Come and sit down. And look in the camera! You always look away. I'd like to interview you.'

'Again? But we did that just yesterday,' I said, sitting down and pouring myself a coffee.

'And what's the topic anyway?' I asked.

'Love,' said Koko. 'Do you know a certain Grasina Kosel?'

Of course I knew the woman, but she lived in Poland and I hadn't heard anything more from her since I left all those years ago. I was badly shaken and couldn't get two sensible words together.

'Grażyna Kozieł?' I stuttered.

'So you do know her...'

'Yes, for heaven's sake, but what about her? Stop fooling around!'

'The old girl left a message for you on the answering machine – couldn't understand a word of it. For us Russians, Polish sounds like birds twittering away on an early summer morning. Terrible!'

I listened to the message several times, in disbelief. She must have gone crazy. Grażyna Kozieł – my first girlfriend, my long lost love – had run off; had left husband and child back in Lidzbark Warmiński, and was now waiting for me to pick her up as quickly as possible from the central train station.

I translated the message for Koko and told him who Grażyna was.

I said, 'How's she got hold of our number – that's what I want to know. From my parents maybe?'

'Uh huh...' said Koko. 'But say we take this lass on – you can hardly tell her after three days, "Go and find somewhere else now." And anyway, the thought of a woman hunting through our cupboards for loose change makes me feel quite weird... On the other hand... Maybe I'll fall in love with her,

and a Pole is, after all, a half Russian! You'll be our witness…
Pani Grasina and I will have Russian-German-Polish babies.
Mongrels! They're the smartest…'

'Koko, shut up! And turn off that stupid camera. This
isn't funny.'

'Ah ha ha ha!' laughed Koko. 'Come on, let's go to the
station and pick up the poor little dove. Let's see what the
gods are trying to tell us with this visit. The trip to Amsterdam's
not going anywhere.'

We got showered and all dressed up: ties, hats and black
jackets, finished off with sunglasses like the Blues Brothers. We
were both only five foot ten and so we always wore shoes
with big heels, mostly black leather boots with toes sharpened
to a point like pencils.

But inside I was reeling: Koko and I had come to an
agreement a few years ago that ladies weren't allowed into our
flat – love sickness belonged out on the streets, in the bars and
in quiet hotel rooms. In our house, peace must reign – women
were a taboo topic within our four walls. What on earth had
suddenly got into us – didn't I dream of a blonde from
Chicago (five foot six and, whatever else, no moles on her
back!), and Koko loved Russians? I looked in the hall mirror,
combed my hair and said: 'We're making a big mistake. Why
bother making any rules, when we don't stick to them?'

'This is an emergency,' replied Koko, and packed the
Canon into a plastic bag. 'You can't just turn your back on
Grasina. After all, she was your first conquest, if I'm not
mistaken.'

As we made our way through the city traffic towards the
centre, Koko drove my fully automatic Tadek-Brozio-Mercedes
and grilled me like a detective: 'Eye colour?'

'Green.'

'Age?'

'Thirty.'

'And how did it start?'

'We were late developers. Two nineteen year-old

greenhorns with no experience.'

'Fantastic!' said Koko. 'But where did you meet each other then?'

'On a sailing tour from Wegorzewo to Mikołajki. We hadn't even set eyes on one another before, even though we lived in the very same town, in Lidzbark Warmiński.'

I wanted to spare Koko the end of my love story, for now at least, because there was nothing nice to report here: sure, I was going to have to tell him sometime, probably even pretty soon, how I came to leave Grażyna.

I turned on the radio. I wanted to remember alone.

After my training as an agricultural engineer and the relevant school exams I was called up for military service. But the order was immediately withdrawn when I claimed to be about to start studying astronomy in Toruń. Only I didn't want to become an astronomer – not for my parents, nor for the People's Republic of Poland, and least of all for myself.

My father, who liked to spend his spare time star gazing through his expensive Made-in-the-GDR-Telescope, had got it into his head that I was a genius, a second Copernicus, because I had always been brilliant at maths and amazed my teachers. But back then I had other plans: sailing, fishing and smoking cigarettes around the camp fire with my mates – that was my astronomy, and nothing else.

But I also hated the idea of brushing my teeth every morning with twenty spotty, big-mouthed lads doing their service, sleeping with them in one room, and most importantly of all: I felt myself entirely unsuitable for defending our Socialist homeland.

So I relieved my parents of one thousand marks to go and start my studies in Toruń and went to see the lawyer Babowski, a dealer in real German papers: he was able, at a small fee, to turn any Masurian Pole into a pureblood German, an ethnic German, so to speak. He told me as soon as I'd found my feet in Germany I should write to my girl and break it off with her, then find myself a rich Hanseatic woman to marry instead.

And I actually did write that letter to Grażyna. Heaven knows why: I still loved her!

I never got a reply.

My parents forgave me my flight, and sometimes even visited me in our high-rise.

But I still couldn't get along with German women, just like Koko. He had become a Communist and a Russian, and I fancied myself to be a notorious dissident, or at least Mister Tadek Brozio from Chicago, someone who owned a barber's in the Polish quarter and played chess with the customers. Sometimes I even imagined that Bremen was in America, especially when I was standing on the balcony of our flat after I'd smoked a joint, Koko had put on the old Pink Floyd or Grateful Dead records and the city lights grew ever larger and brighter, like supernovas.

'Tadek, wake up,' said Koko, 'We're here.'

He parked the car right in front of the train station. I placed the 'PRESS' sign prominently on the dashboard, a trick that usually saved us a few marks, then off we went.

Koko turned on his video camera. We wandered around the station forecourt for a while, ate a hot dog and smoked cigarettes. But I couldn't find Grażyna anywhere. All sorts of women hurried past, each one more beautiful than the last; it almost made me dizzy. What did they all want, I wondered, and who loved them? Why didn't a single man approach them?

'Tadek, open your eyes,' said Koko. 'She must be here somewhere. Look! That woman over there in the telephone booth with the leopard skin. Is that her?'

'I don't know,' I answered. 'Her pointed nose... Her knock-knees...'

We ordered another sausage and washed it down with a can of beer. It was our lunch.

Then Koko said, 'I could do with a coffee now. In any case, we're not leaving without Grasina. If it comes to it, we'll stay the night here.'

'Koko,' I said, 'She's called Graschina! Get it right! Maybe she's taken a taxi and is sitting on the stairs crying outside our flat. What do you think? What would you do in her place?'

'Well, I'm trying to think myself into her shoes.'

I braced myself, because if Koko had a talent, it was for making mountains out of molehills.

He said, 'Look. Here's a woman who loved you. You dump her and disappear. You jerk! Well anyway. She gets married when she's twenty-one, 'cos some guy's got her pregnant, which is par for the course in your hovel of a town. But this guy has money. He deals in little Christmas trees, exporting them to Germany and Sweden, or he smuggles uranium out of the Ukraine and into the West. Doesn't matter what he does. The main thing is, it makes dough. In any case, he's a big hero in Lidzbark. But Graschina can't sleep. She can't stop thinking about Tadek Brozio, who once upon a time promised her the earth… who's living in Bremen now… "Whatever happened to him?" she asks herself…. "Is he a millionaire now?"'

I said, 'That's enough, Koko. We're going home. I have to listen to that message again.'

'Oh, I can't wait!' he said. 'That'll be a great scene: Tadek Brozio kneels down in front of the answering machine, close to a nervous breakdown! You're driving, I'm the cameraman.'

Before we drove home we did another round of the station forecourt, as if we were border control officers. We went on to every platform and even asked the information point to call out Grażyna's name over the loudspeaker system, and two Poles came to us.

When they went away looking disappointed, Koko said to me, 'What were they expecting? That we propose to them?'

Then we dragged ourselves to the car park; it was raining and neither of us spoke. Koko gave me the car keys.

On the way home Koko fished a tape out of the glove

compartment that I only listened to when times were really tough: the double album 'The Wall' – this music was perfect for mourning, and my unspoken wish had always been that at least one song from this album should be played at my funeral. Koko didn't know anything about that though. He put the tape in and turned the volume to half eleven. I completely lost it.

I shouted: 'Do you want to kill me? I'm in no mood to die right now!'

'Yet again, we've failed…' Koko replied.

'Firstly, my dear friend – Grażyna doesn't know you – I'm the one she's looking for!'

'Oh right. Wonderful! Now I know. You don't need me anymore. You think I know nothing about women.'

I didn't see any point in continuing the conversation. I turned the music down and looked for a distraction, anything to help me forget it all (Grażyna's call, Koko's interpretation of my love story, the winter rain I hated so much) – and I turned to a tried and tested method that always helped me relax a little: I picked at my teeth with a match, clicked my tongue and hissed loudly like a locomotive.

Koko said: 'Stop being so disgusting. I can't stand it! I know exactly what you're thinking right now. You want me to shut my gob. But I'm not going to! God help me! I'm not going to tuck in my tail and tell you you can just forget about your Graschina…'

'Koko! Everyone has a skeleton in the cupboard,' I replied. 'I hardly need to tell you that… Think of all your Russians… I don't want to know just how many sons and daughters you have, for example…'

'You mean I should start counting?' he asked. 'I don't get it…'

'You stupid Russian! If at least you actually were one. We were planning to go to Amsterdam and get ourselves well and truly tanked up, and now I'm supposed to scrap all that and go looking for a needle in a haystack. You saw for yourself –

she wasn't there!'

My friend didn't say anything more. He pressed the stop button. He'd got another tape of material. He was happy, although he didn't want to admit it. There wasn't a single director who could measure up to him, and the kind of cinemas where his films would run hadn't yet been built. They would have to have oversized screens, screens of cosmic proportions, where every single earthling could watch his own story.

Translated from the German by Rebecca Braun

Silver Rain

PAWEŁ HUELLE

To Zbigniew Żakiewicz

Anusewicz was no great believer in prophetic dreams, Sibylline oracles or palmistry. And yet, when he woke up that day bathed in sweat and gasping for breath he felt that something must be going to happen. Nina, aged twenty, beautiful and alluring, had been dancing in a meadow, as if specially for him. He walked towards her slowly, feeling the soft blades of grass tickling his feet. They embraced passionately, suddenly naked like Adam and Eve under the apple tree. He felt an intense spasm of pleasure as he pressed his lips to her full breasts. Straight after that, God knows why or what for, Father Wołkonowicz had appeared in the meadow. In a patched cassock and shabby shoes, with drops of sweat on his brow, he was roaring and thundering the words of Isaiah about the Earth and its immoral inhabitants being burned to ashes. But why a moment later had all three of them ended up in a palatial ballroom? And what was the military band in German uniform that was playing to them from the courtyard supposed to mean? Now wearing a starched shirt front and an impeccably cut tail-coat Father Wołkonowicz was waltzing with Nina, dressed like a bride, while he, Anusewicz, went after them, also to the rhythm of a waltz, through deserted halls and galleries, down corridors and staircases.

The dream had no clear end. For some time Anusewicz gazed at the ceiling, and he wasn't sure if it was his flat, or that strangely empty, unfamiliar palace. As soon as he got up and caught sight of himself in the mirror, he felt profound disappointment. In the meadow his body had been supple and agile. In the real world to which he had returned, it offered a rather discouraging sight. His sagging pot belly, the grey tufts of sparse hair on his head and his drooping shoulders were a pitiless reminder of the years gone by. The magical, rejuvenating power of the dream appealed to him very much. Over breakfast it occurred to him that he hadn't felt desire for several years at least. But why Nina? And why Father Wołkonowicz? The Russians had deported her right at the start, in 1939. The Germans had shot Father Wołkonowicz as a hostage three years later. In fact, all trace of Nina had been lost. Had she died in a camp? Had she left Siberia with Anders' Army and ended her days many years later in London, or in sunny California? What could it matter nowadays... Where were they now?

As he left the house, Anusewicz kept repeating this question over and over, and it caused him pain. He did in fact believe deeply in the immortality of the soul, but did that automatically entail the resurrection of the body? Was it really quite so certain? If a body that had crumbled to dust could return to its former shape, he might not only see Nina again one day, but that entire long-dead world. Vistas through the pine trees at dawn, sheets spread to dry in the meadows, the larch-wood beams of the house at Rudzieńszczyzna, his father in riding boots, or a snowflake on his mother's fur collar. But does God bother with such trivia? There was plenty to imply that He had a hundred times more serious troubles, from hurtling, disintegrating galaxies, via endless wars, to volcanoes and common floods.

Anusewicz passed the brewery, and in the passage under the electric railway tracks he bought three purple roses. As he boarded the tram he felt sure his dream hadn't appeared by accident. The presence of Father Wołkonowicz was proof of that. A cleric, no matter what his denomination, always means some sort of change. Perhaps when he got home from the theatre he'd find a letter from Nina in the post box? That would be a surprise. 'I'm coming in a month and I must see your grandchildren.' Some miraculous escapes, years of hunger and hoping against hope; yes, they'd have something to talk about over a carafe of dogberry vodka. But as he got off the tram not far from the Uphagen mansion, he came to the conclusion that he wouldn't want to see Nina old and wrinkled, not even with an American set of false teeth. The Nina he had seen in his dream was immortal and happy. The one he would greet on the threshold of his flat would only be a poor copy, an imitation of that one. But he had no time for further reflections. As ever, he presented the flowers to Miss Andruszkiewicz, and as ever, she gave him the key to the storeroom.

In pitch darkness Anusewicz felt for the spotlight switch, and a focused stream of light shifted along the shelves and pegs, picking the puppets' immobile heads and bodies out of the darkness. Sindbad the Sailor had his glassy eye on Alice, Dratewka the Cobbler was curled up next to Big Ears, a sad Ali Baba was leaning his chin on Grandpa Utopek the lighthouse-keeper, and a Little Owl with floppy wings was perching on Pinocchio's nose like a roosting hen. Anusewicz had brought their gestures, their trials and tribulations and their funny little catchphrases to life many times, lending them his voice and hand movements. Now that he was retired, he came here once a month, and in the total silence he acted out his own improvised scenes with them. Sometimes the Wicked Stepmother spoke the words of Lady Macbeth, or Johnny Dunderhead waved his arms about and spouted the same twaddle as the old and new politicians.

Without a second thought, Anusewicz took a white-armed, sheet-wearing Grim Reaper from the rack. He untangled the strings, adjusted the fastening of the silver scythe and made him patter to and fro, as if on stage. He snapped his great big teeth just as he should, and rattled his scythe like mad. But Anusewicz wasn't happy with something. Only when the Grim Reaper started tap dancing to the rhythm of the swing he was softly whistling, did he smile at him and say:

'Now I can see it, old man, you've got a great future ahead of you.'

The Grim Reaper spread his arms and bowed politely to the invisible audience. But that was all. No new idea, no improvisation or funny sketch occurred to Anusewicz. He usually spent an hour here, sometimes more, without looking at his watch, but this time every minute was dragging on unbearably. On top of that he had an unpleasant feeling, as though in the darkness beyond the bright shaft of the spotlight, four eyes were watching him: those of Nina and Father Wołkonowicz. When he put on the overhead lamp, he didn't feel any better, because there was another thought that wouldn't stop pestering him – that someone connected with this morning's dream was waiting for him at home, while he was wasting his time here to no purpose.

'Better cut it short,' he said out loud. 'The worst thing is uncertainty.'

Somewhat surprised, Miss Andruszkiewicz packed the Grim Reaper in a plastic bag for him and, without the usual chat, he set off for the tram stop. What was he going home for? A dream was just a dream, nothing but a stupid nightmare. He could easily stay at the theatre. The inspiration would come at the right moment, yes, it was sure to.

And indeed, the letterbox was quite empty, there was no scrap of paper shoved in the door, and without his wife bustling about or his grandchildren's hullabaloo the flat seemed unnaturally quiet. Anusewicz shambled into the kitchen, and then, as he drank a cold Elbląg beer he stood the Grim Reaper on his desk. Among the family photographs, books and notes, without any scenery or spotlights he looked quite harmless. Anusewicz's fingers took hold of the strings again, and sounding suitably strident, he recited:

> *O my noble ancient Sire,*
> *The world makes noise 'til it doth tire,*
> *The young man can, the old must try*
> *To bolt, or else he'll choke and die.*

The Grim Reaper made his robe rustle, rapped his scythe and sang the next couplet in a different, maybe slightly Belarussian accent:

> *My crown and sceptre I'd concede*
> *If from death's dance I could be freed.*
> *What bitter tears an old man weeps*
> *As death's grim ballet jumps and leaps.*

The big wooden boots tapped on the desktop. Anusewicz purred in satisfied agreement, but the next couplet remained unspoken. This was because of Mr Winterhaus, who just at that moment knocked at the front door. With the Grim Reaper resting on his arm, Anusewicz rather reluctantly opened it, and for a while both gentlemen stood looking at each other in silence.

'I am Vinterhaus,' said Winterhaus. 'May I please talk vith you?'

'Naturally,' replied Anusewicz, and led his guest into the dining room.

But there was nothing natural about it.

'There's a bit of a problem, as there alvays is with this sort of conversation,' sighed Winterhaus, 'but I couldn't put it off any longer. You know? I've been up these stairs three times before und run avay. I vas afraid.'

'Of me?' asked Anusewicz in amazement.

'Of the situation. You know? I used to live here. Until the end of the var.'

'Oh, I see,' said Anusewicz. 'That's interesting.'

The man didn't look like the typical German, though his well-groomed grey hair combined with his gold-rimmed spectacles, not to mention his accent, spoke for themselves.

'Do you want to take some pictures?' asked Anusewicz,

after an awkward silence. 'Look round the rooms? There aren't many of the old things left. The mirror in the bathroom, the shoe cupboard, nothing else. You must know,' he went on, a little irritated, 'I wasn't the first tenant. There was a clerk from the Poznań area here before me, and before him there was a tailor, a Jew. The tailor moved out in 1947, to some suburb of Wrzeszcz, the clerk got a promotion to Warsaw, and then I moved in. It was, just a moment, let me think… yes, it was in 1949, in May. What else do you want to know?'

'This is no ordinary matter,' said Winterhaus hesitantly. 'I don't vant any photographs or souvenirs, nothing. I came here because of my father. I kept having the same incredible dream. You know? He left treasure in the kitchen dresser that stood next to the stove. All his life he kept saying: 'Helmut, it must be there.' But I did not believe him. Und ven he died, every night I dreamed about the dresser und the coins. Every night. Und then I suffered from *Schlaflosigkeit*, und the doctor told me: "Vhy don't you go there, Herr Vinterhaus, and make sure there's no dresser, no treasure, nothing there."'

Anusewicz wiped the sweat from his brow. He couldn't remember a kitchen dresser. The stove, of course, with the metal hotplate, stood in the kitchen for many years until the gas was connected. But a dresser? The only dresser had been in the dining room, here, where the storage unit now stood and the television. He had sold it for a song, in 1971 or 2. It had cloudy glass doors and scratched veneer in an awful cherry colour. But the question of the coins interested him greatly.

'So was there a lot of it?' he asked. 'Gold, I guess?'

'Oh, I don't know,' said Winterhaus. 'You know, he collected those coins that vere minted in Danzig – that is, in Gdansk,' he corrected himself, 'vithout letting my mother, me or my brother know about it. He vas alvays increasing his collection. The more of them he had, the greater his fear that she vould find out he kept spending money on them. Und he vas so afraid that ven the time came to escape, he couldn't get them out, because she vould have seen vhat he'd been spending money on for so many years. You understand?'

'I do. But did you ever see the coins?'

'Never.'

'What about your mother? Or your brother?'

'They never did either. Und aftervards no one vould believe him. It was only this dream of mine, und then the doctor, as I told you.'

'There are all sorts of dreams,' said Anusewicz. 'Today for instance I dreamed I was in the meadow at our Rudzieńszczyzna. I'm sure you don't know where that is.'

'No.'

'In the East,' sighed Anusewicz. 'It's in Belarus now.'

Winterhaus nodded sympathetically. But he didn't look upset, at least not for that reason. He followed his host into the kitchen and was happy to accept a beer. He showed where the dresser had stood and described exactly what it had been like.

'Oh!' cried Anusewicz. 'You said the dresser, the dresser, but it was a kitchen cupboard – in three parts, right?'

'Right.'

'And which one were the coins hidden in?'

'In the middle bit, the biggest. That's vhat my father said. Und that's vhat I dreamed.'

'Benek!' exclaimed Anusewicz. 'Oh yes, Benek! But has he still got it?'

And before Winterhaus had had time to say another word, Anusewicz had put on his shoes, thrown his jacket over his shoulders and commanded:

'Let's go, Mr Winterhaus, quickly.'

At this point there was a slight controversy. Winterhaus suggested they take a taxi, and that he would pay. But Anusewicz refused to agree to that, and doggedly insisted on taking the tram, which – as always in such cases – didn't come for ages.

'Who is Benek?' asked Winterhaus at last.

'He's Bernard, my brother-in-law, my wife's brother,' explained Anusewicz.

Then he added that the cupboard in question, or to be precise, its biggest, middle bit, had long since been given to Bernard, who had got married to Barbara and needed furniture.

'He's either thrown it out, or he's got it somewhere in the cellar,' Anusewicz pondered aloud. 'But what if he found it?'

At this point Anusewicz remembered how Bernard had surprised everyone a few years ago by suddenly buying a car. Where had he got so much money from out of the blue? But he didn't mention it to Winterhaus. In the crowded tram the conversation flagged, and when they boarded a bus near the Upland Gate and headed towards Orunia, Winterhaus said in a hushed tone:

'You know vhat? I'm not concerned about the money, the property. I just vanted to check if my father vas telling the truth or not. Und that dream, if you please. Do you believe in dreams? Und then the *Schlaflosigkeit* – er, insomnia.'

'Hmm,' mumbled Anusewicz, 'some dreams portend something, they tell us something. Others are meaningless, just idiotic. And who'd know the difference?'

The bus stopped by the Radunia Canal, in the shade of some old trees. As they got out, to their right the old Jesuit church rose from the hills, while to their left the gently sloping upland declined more and more slowly into a completely flat depression, cut across by canals and a patchwork of fields. They headed left, passing some poor, rented apartment blocks, some small factories, warehouses and railway tracks, until finally, under the shade of some chestnut trees, the cobblestones came to an end, and they went into a field road.

'My father,' said Winterhaus, 'vas an official at the Danziger Strassenbahn, that is the electric trams. Tovards the end of the var they made him the director.'

'And mine,' said Anusewicz, 'had Rudzieńszczyzna. Not much land, but a lot of forests, sawmills, a watermill, lakes...'

'He didn't go to the var,' Winterhaus continued, 'because he vas lame, in the right leg.'

'Neither did mine,' explained Anusewicz, 'because he was too old. But the Soviets took him and he never came back. Never. Then, when the Germans came, they shot Uncle Witold, and I was left alone with my mother.'

'Und my older brother,' added Winterhaus, 'vas killed at Kursk. The Führer sent a letter und a posthumous *kreuz*.'

'I was an only child,' said Anusewicz.

Both gentlemen walked the last stretch of road across the weir in silence. Bernard's cottage was by the canal, among mouldering willows, burdock leaves and grass that no one had mown. In the yard lay the wreck of an old truck, some rusty sheets of metal, some bricks from a demolished building, and some rolls of wire. The nose of a punt was poking out of a dense clump of nettles; full of holes, it had been taken over by the hens.

'Don't say anything,' Anusewicz warned. 'I'll do the talking.'

Barbara was making soup. The children were on holiday, near Kościerzyna, and Benek, so she said, was out driving the taxi. Anusewicz came straight to the point. Did Barbara remember that white cupboard they'd brought them from Wrzeszcz by horse and cart? It was two days after the wedding, when they moved into this ruin and started renovating it.

'How could I fail to remember?' laughed Barbara. 'You boys drank for three days on end – you, Benek and that carter, Bieszke – and I had to feed his old nag and patch the roof because it was pouring. Men,' she snorted. 'You lot are never any use.'

Anusewicz waved his hands. Why remind him of those things? The point was the cupboard from the flat on Gołębia Street. This gentleman, Mr Winterhaus, had come from Germany looking for some family documents and photographs.

They had to help him, because they were probably hidden in that cupboard…'

'*Was ist verloren?*' said Barbara to Mr Winterhaus.

'Oh, I can speak Polish,' he replied, bowing and kissing her hand. 'My grandmother taught me Polish, because she vas a Pole, though her surname vas Kosterke.'

'Where is that cupboard? Have you still got it somewhere?' pressed Anusewicz. 'We'll take a look and be on our way, it's no great bother. You see, Barbara, Mr Winterhaus used to live in our flat, what I meant to say is, we live where he used to, and when the Ruskies came he didn't have time to take everything with him. In that cupboard there were…'

'…some Tsarist roubles,' laughed Barbara, 'a pile of gold. Will you take it with you? There'll be a bit less mould in the junk heap. It's there, in the shed by the canal. I'm making dinner – will you have some soup afterwards?'

Anusewicz cleared his throat affirmatively and, leading Winterhaus across the yard, headed for the tin box of a garage that Barbara so generously called the shed. Indeed, it was chock-full of junk. Apart from carpenter's tools, empty crates, withered boat ribs, car parts, hoes, spades, canvas sacks, bottles and jam jars there were also several broken stools, a chair full of holes, a ripped sofa, a clapped-out moped, a children's wicker pushchair, some skis, a small cast-iron stove, hooks and lines for catching eels, a radio in an ebonite box, as well as a chipped bidet and an easel.

'Oh!' said Winterhaus. 'This is something!'

'But where's the cupboard?' said Anusewicz, flapping his arms about helplessly. 'I can't see it anywhere.'

It took them a while to notice it: a piece of cloth of a sky-blue colour, with a white dove and the inscription 'PEACE-MIR'. The dove was holding a twig in its beak, though it was hard to tell if it was an olive one, and the whole drawing was ringed by a symbolic laurel wreath.

'Well,' said Anusewicz, tearing the banner off the cupboard, 'we've got you at last! Where should it be?'

'Here, at the bottom,' said Winterhaus, pointing. 'Ve've got to remove the first layer of the floor. That's vhat I dreamed. Und that's vhat my father said.'

They found a chisel and some hammers and rapidly got down to work. Under the first layer of plywood there was a second, then yet another one, and finally to the amazed Anusewicz, and the no less amazed Winterhaus, several rows of narrow compartments appeared, in which the coins lay wrapped in bandages, like the beads on an abacus. Every crack had been stuffed with cotton wool and then filled with putty.

'Your dad was a pretty good conspirator,' said Anusewicz, digging out one bundle after another. 'You could have turned this box upside down and even then nothing would have rattled. Look, look, here are some bigger ones…'

They made space on a carpentry table and laid out the little round parcels one after another. Once they had extracted the last one, Anusewicz patted Winterhaus on the back and added:

'You start.'

With trembling fingers, Winterhaus unwound the first rag. A silver coin the size of a dollar fell onto the table.

'Well I never, well I never,' whispered Anusewicz. The reverse showed Christ in a long robe, holding a royal orb; around him ran the imprecation, "DEFENDE NOS CHRISTE SALVATOR." On the obverse there were two lions rampant, holding up the emblem of the city, entwined with the inscription, "MONETA NOVA CIVI GEDANENSIS." Above the animals' manes there was also a date: 1577.

'It's from a time of var,' stated Winterhaus. 'Instead of the Polish king they minted it vith the image of Jesus.'

'War, yes, yes, war,' said Anusewicz, unwinding the next bit of rag, from which he extracted a small coin, clearly considerably older, because it had a very worn-out face. 'And what might this one be?'

Winterhaus took off his glasses, used the left lens as a

magnifying glass, and said:

'This is the coin of a Pomeranian duke. You see the griffin? Oh, it says here: "DANCEKE DOMINI ZWANTOPELK." Take a look.'

Once he had positioned the lens at the right distance, Anusewicz positively whistled in admiration. With his proudly unfurled standard and shield of the House of Griffins, the Kashubian Duke Świętopełk was spurring on his horse.

'In those days,' he muttered, 'my ancestors still worshipped sacred serpents.'

But Winterhaus hadn't heard him. As he undid the next few bundles, onto the table fell jingling groshy, thalers, half thalers, three-groshy coins and ducats, and it looked like silver rain, with a chance piece of gold glittering here and there among them. The Jagiellonians, the Saxons, the Waza Kings and the Griffins, Prussian Commanders and Electors all lay beside each other amicably now, as if they had never been divided by drawn swords, battlefields, customs duties, intrigue, treacherous murders and battleships sunk at the bottom of the bay. There were no duplicates. Only a five-ducat piece with the head of King Władysław and a panorama of the city on the reverse featured in three, non-identical specimens.

'*Schlaflosigkeit*,' sighed Winterhaus contentedly, 'I don't think I'm going to suffer from it any more.'

'Oh no, surely not.' Anusewicz was restoring the cupboard to its former appearance. 'But how will you export it all? You have to have special permission. Are there any documents confirming ownership? Because if not, you might have a problem.'

'Oh, I hadn't thought about that at all. You know? The main thing is, I've checked up on my dream. Now I know my father vasn't a madman.'

'You're not going to give them to a museum, are you?'

'A museum? Vhy not? The Tramdriver Vinterhaus Collection – it could be very famous.'

This gentle dispute would probably have rambled on, if

the agitated Bernard hadn't come crashing into the tin hut as if pursued by fire.

'Oh, wow.' He let out a long whistle. 'What fine documents you've found in *my* cupboard. And she believed you were looking for some photographs, the stupid woman.' He tapped his forehead. 'I knew you were up to something in here, so I dash down, and there you have it – there's something going on behind my back. I'm Benek,' he offered Winterhaus his hand. 'Taxicab at your service.'

'Vinterhaus,' said Winterhaus.

'Now don't go over the top,' said Anusewicz, trying to appease his brother-in-law. 'That cupboard wasn't mine or yours.'

Bernard couldn't tear his eyes from the coins. He picked them up, inspected them and moved them from place to place.

'Really? In that case, whose was it? As Mr Winterhaus didn't take it with him, first it belonged to the Jew, then that chap from Poznań, and then you. And you gave it to me. Simple, eh? Clear as day. There should be a finder's reward, surely. I don't want anyone to lose. What do you think, *her* Winterhaus?'

'Vell, qvite, qvite, I do not know your law. I think Mister Bernard should receive something. Mister Anusevicz too. Though on the other hand I think this is a complete collection. Do you understand me, gentlemen? I think here there are *alles* the coins minted in Danzig – in Gdansk,' he corrected himself, 'from Duke Świętopełk to the Free City. I propose offering you three thousand marks to share, *gut*?'

'Three thousand marks? In the commie era that was real money,' said Bernard, turning a Saxon Elector's ducat in his hand, 'but nowadays? Nowadays you couldn't buy a new car for that.'

'What is it that makes you Kashubians even more rapacious than vultures?' Anusewicz let loose. 'Come on, Benek, where's our sense of honour? Where's our sense of honour?'

'You lay off the Kashubians! Just look at him, barefoot Antek from beyond the River Bug. A noble gesture, eh? The nobles drained Poland dry long ago, and now the sun shines out of their arses. Fancied themselves as "brothers and gentlemen", ha ha ha!'

'Yes? Yes?' Anusewicz jumped up, gobbling like a turkeycock. 'And who sided with the Germans? Who murdered Leszek the White?'

'Someone vas murdered?' asked Winterhaus, shifting nervously from foot to foot. 'That is politics, do not qvarrel, do not qvarrel.'

But the brothers-in-law weren't listening to their guest any more, just to their own hot blood. Bernard could put up with a lot aimed at himself and his compatriots, but never the idea of ascribing the murder of the Polish Prince Leszek to the Kashubian Duke Świętopełk. Whereas Anusewicz could turn a deaf ear to the remarks about barefoot Antek and a noble gesture, but never to such a base insinuation that the nobles, the brothers and gentlemen, had drunk away the old Poland. And so it began. First with a shove, which led to an exchange of blows.

When Barbara came into the shed, she saw her husband and Anusewicz on the floor, locked together in a wrestling clinch. Clutching his head in both hands, Winterhaus was running around the brothers-in-law repeating:

'*Alles in Ordnung! Alles in Ordnung!* Vhy this *Lärm*? Vhy this *Krawall*? I vill give four thousand marks. Four und a half thousand!'

But that didn't help at all, nor did Barbara's shouts and pushes. The fight was no longer about the money, but about which would come out on top – the Kashubian hot-headedness or the Borderlands quick temper? Which heraldic emblem – the winged Griffin of Pomerania or the mounted Chaser of Pahonia? And it's impossible to say where it would have ended if not for Barbara. Her practical, female reason prompted a simple, effective solution. She ran out of the shed for a moment and came back armed with a rubber garden hose. A jet of cold water soon made the brothers-in-law stop fighting. They spluttered as they wiped their faces, where there wasn't a trace of satisfaction to be seen.

'In five minutes I'm going to serve the dinner, and I don't want to hear a word about this,' said the arbitrator, pointing at the coins.

And so the first spoonfuls of beetroot soup went down their throats in total silence. The only sound to creep onto the veranda and interrupt the clatter of cutlery and discreet slurping was the whistling of swallows, as they flitted between the eaves of the house and the canal. Mr Winterhaus glanced at Anusewicz's black eye and Bernard's torn shirt, then again at the spreading maple, in whose shade a swaggering cockerel was preening his magnificent feathers.

'*Ja*,' he said at last, downing a glass of plain vodka, 'my father vas a strange man. That tram,' he mused, 'the night tram that vas blown up by a bomb...'

'Was it a barricade tram?' asked Anusewicz. 'I saw some of those the year after the war, buried in rubble.'

The eel fricassee served before the main course delayed Mr Winterhaus' answer a bit, though in fact it wasn't an answer, but a story that he only interrupted to dig out bones, clink glasses and make lip-smacking noises.

That night before the attack, when the Russian artillery were cleaning the barrels of their cannon and calculating their trajectories, Direktor Winterhaus made his way to the tram depot and roamed around the empty halls, immobile points and switched-off lamps; and when he came upon the last tramcar that had not been militarised, he hopped aboard, raised the bow collector and set off for the city, remembering the old days when he was still an ordinary tram driver. First he travelled the No 3 route, then the No 5, and next the 7, halting at all the stops and calling out their names; and he drove like that from Friedenschloss to Weichselbahnhof, from

Broesen to Ohra and Emaus, changing the points himself at the sidings and punching the tickets; and the Schupo and SS night patrols saluted him, because the prudent Direktor Winterhaus had put a picture of the Führer in the front window of the tram between two oil lamps, like in a Catholic church, so they thought it was a propaganda run to keep up the fighting spirit, which was highly recommended, which was sorely needed, as there were already deserters and defeatists hanging from the hundred-year-old boughs along Grosse Allee, with signs on their chests reading: 'I refused to die for the Führer and the Fatherland', and their shoes rapped against the tramcar windows like drops of March rain or sleet; and like this Direktor Winterhaus's tram flashed down the defiles between buildings, past parks and along the city avenues, right up to the moment when the ground shook and the first shells hit the Lower Town and Granary Island, right up to the moment when great tongues of flame began to consume the red Gothic of the Hanseatic League; and that was when Direktor Winterhaus threw the picture of the Führer in the mud, blew out the oil lamps and hung a white sheet on the tramcar, but it wasn't much help, because the tramlines had already been torn up, ripped apart by grenades, and he couldn't go any further, so he jumped off the tram and ran for home; and just then a shell exploded behind him, and the last civilian tram in the city of Danzig flew into thousands of tiny pieces of glass, metal and wood, and Direktor Winterhaus stopped, shocked by this sudden transformation, and realised that this was the absolute end of his tramcar career, which he had started as an assistant mechanic, and the absolute end of this city, which would never be what it had been again.

'Beautiful,' sighed Anusewicz. 'The shoes of the hanged defeatists peeking in the windows, and that white sheet.'

'I can't see anything beautiful in that,' cut in Bernard, getting down to some chops, like everyone else. 'They got it up the arse because they deserved it. But that was too little.

Too little. They should have all been sent to Siberia as Stalin wanted.'

'It is very cold there,' said Winterhaus.

This matter-of-fact comment prompted general merriment at the table. They joked about the Russians and Siberia for a good while, and once the vodka and puddings were finished, Bernard tapped the homemade wine, and amid the buzzing of flies and the chirping of cicadas, the warm afternoon by the canal took on its full bucolic splendour.

To this day no one knows who hit upon the idea of the boating escapade. Was it Anusewicz, who was thinking back to the boats on Saint John's Eve at Rudzieńszczyzna? Or Bernard, who had fished in Kashubia since childhood? Or maybe Mr Winterhaus, whose memory prompted some rather vague images of stone sluices, drawbridges and canals as the landscape of this part of the city? In any case, it came out of nowhere. As she bustled around the table, Barbara suddenly noticed that the three gentlemen, who shortly before were dozing in their cane armchairs, had disappeared from the veranda. Their voices, loud and cheerful, were now coming from the water's edge. She ran over there and saw Bernard and Anusewicz dragging a rubber dinghy out of the shed.

'You must be mad!' she cried. 'Going fishing in that state? There's no question of it.'

But her female spirit, wanting to curb the spirit of the restless men once again that day, had to give way, because a boyish spirit craving variety and adventure had jointly entered the three gentlemen.

'What fishing?' growled Bernard. 'We just want a bit of a ride, to cool off.'

'Yes, yes,' added Anusewicz. 'The view of the city from this side is unusual.'

Finally, once the army dinghy had been inflated and Bernard had fixed an outboard motor to the stern, the gentlemen got on board. Barbara managed to hand them a thermos of coffee and some shortbread from the jetty, just in case. For a while the engine refused to fire up, and the dinghy spun around its own axis.

'What a bloody load of crap,' Bernard ranted. 'I haven't used it since last year.'

But this obstacle gave way too. After the umpteenth tug at the rope, the air was rent apart by a dreadful roar, and then amid a cloud of petrol fumes and a whirring noise the dinghy moved forward majestically, cutting across a green curtain of duckweed. Leaning out over the semicircular prow, Anusewicz commanded:

'Go right, Bernard, right I say, there are some bits of old stakes in the middle.'

Bernard nodded agreeably, but his brother-in-law's warnings didn't unduly bother him. He knew every bit of sunken scrap metal and every dangerous tree root on these waters. It wasn't for nothing that he'd fished for eels here, in every legitimate and illegitimate way. Finally, once they had sailed along the river to the sluice, as he gazed at the bastions covered in reeds, grass and burdock, Mr Winterhaus said:

'I vas here on a picnic with my father. But it looked completely different then.'

'Yes,' explained Bernard. 'Nowadays you can't sail into the city this way. The sluice isn't navigable. But we can carry the dinghy to the other side – in fact why don't we?'

Not without some mild puffing and panting, the three gentlemen carried the rubber boat across a bank of earth, over the stone rim surrounding the sluice, and dropped it back into the water beside the bindweed-choked ruins of a building that looked like an old granary. The view they now had in sight delighted Winterhaus in particular. In a dense tunnel of greenery, there before them lay the brown thread of the Motława river, reflecting the Gothic brickwork of church and town hall towers among the clouds.

'I have made a decision – I brought ze treasure,' said Winterhaus, and to Anusewicz and Bernard's amazement, from his inside jacket pocket he brought out a little canvas sack, with the old coins jingling inside it like a heavily laden swarm of bees getting ready for flight. Anusewicz and Bernard exchanged glances, but there was no time to investigate why Winterhaus had brought the money with him, or when and in what imperceptible way he had done it.

As the motorised dinghy sailed under the bridge at Elbląska Street and passed the ugly tower blocks on Kamienna Grobla, the landing stage and the old granaries on Chmielna Street, Mr Winterhaus took his father's coins out of the grey bag at random, and sorted them into three piles, monotonously chanting:

'This is for me, this is for Mr Benek, this is for Anusevicz. This is for me, this is for Mr Benek, this is for Anusevicz.'

Unseen, they slipped past Ołowianka, and at the level of the Polish Hook, where instead of embankments, granaries and buildings, huge ships' hulls began to surround them, Anusewicz felt worried that they may have gone too far, and may not be allowed to sail here in such a cockleshell, especially one made of rubber. Bernard was of a different opinion: they'd go and see the walls of the fortress and then turn back level with the monument, because if you want an outing, that's an outing, and as for navigation, he used to sail here ten years ago on the pusher-tug 'Buhaj' and knew every buoy here, as well as all the customs men and the port police. As they reached Westerplatte, Mr Winterhaus finished dividing the coins and handed the brothers-in-law their shares of the treasure.

'We must celebrate this,' said Benek, extracting a hip flask from his inside pocket. 'Well, here's to reconciliation. Look over there, Mr Winterhaus – that's the monument to our heroes, they were the first people in Europe, Mr Winterhaus, to tell Hitler: *No pasaran.*'

'Oh yes, I know it vasn't like Czechoslovakia here – ve could even hear those shots at our house.'

'And that's where the battleship Schleswig-Holstein was moored,' said Anusewicz, pointing.

'On a nice, friendly visit, *herzlich willkommen!*' added

Bernard, turning the rudder so that the dinghy described a wide semicircle and was now sailing towards the city.

The little tin cup from the hip flask did the rounds smoothly from hand to hand, and soon the harbour smell of grease, rather dirty water and fish was mixed with the aroma of the coffee that Anusewicz poured into a mug from Barbara's thermos.

'A beautiful day, a beautiful day,' repeated Winterhaus. 'I never dreamed about anything like this.'

'Life is more beautiful than dreams,' said Anusewicz confidently, 'as you can see for yourself.'

He was going to add something else, but the dreamy Winterhaus began to chant in a pure, strong voice:

Das Wandern ist des Müllers Lust,

das Wandern, das Wandern

and tossed his head to encourage the brothers-in-law to join in with him, at which Anusewicz and Bernard chorused:

das Wandern, das Wandern

at which Winterhaus even more joyfully jumped to the first line of the second verse:

Vom Wasser haben wir's gelernt

and in a now perfectly harmonised trio all the sailors chorused:

Vom Wasser haben wir's gelernt,

vom Wasser, vom Wasser.

And although it wasn't a rushing stream, beside which there should have been a mill and a half-timbered house, but a port canal, where from the banks instead of fir trees steel cranes shot into the sky, at that moment all three really did feel like wanderers descending from the mountains and coming across an enchanting, isolated farmhouse, and there inside...

However, the song was never finished. At the words about the master and the mistress, something grated on the port side, hissed and puffed, and seconds later the dinghy began to sink surprisingly quickly in the dark-green swirl of the Motława. Bernard didn't even have time to unhitch the motor, which with a hiss and a gurgle dragged the floppy sheet of rubber to the bottom.

'Jesus Christ, Mr Winterhaus! Can you swim?' cried Anusewicz.

But doggy-paddling in hectic circles, Winterhaus hadn't heard the question, though he kept repeating:

'*Mein Gott, mein Gott*, all is lost, *alles*.'

And indeed, there was nothing to save. The little sack containing Winterhaus' coins and the plastic bag filled with Bernard's share had gone to the bottom just as rapidly as the dinghy burdened with its motor. Only Anusewicz, who had parcelled out his portion among all his jacket pockets, had not lost anything, but when they started swimming towards the quay, all this ballast weighed him down dreadfully. He kicked off his shoes, and once he had recovered a bit of vigour after the initial shock, he tried using one hand to empty his brimfull pockets. But it wasn't easy. His jacket had gone as stiff as armour, and Anusewicz found that he was having more and more difficulty keeping above the surface. Finally, with immense effort, he pulled first his left, then his right arm out of the sleeves, and now, very much lighter, he was the last to swim to shore.

Struggling and striving, they finally overcame the slimy ledge protruding from the quay. They lay on the grass and stared at the sky in silence.

'It has all drownded,' said Winterhaus at last.

'When I get hold of the Ruski who sold me that army surplus boat, I'll smash his face in,' threatened Bernard.

They got up and went on their way, Winterhaus holding one salvaged shoe, Bernard barefoot, and Anusewicz in grey socks. While the shade of the chestnut trees and the walls of the warehouses on Wiosna Ludów Street, where they had landed, were still protecting them, they didn't yet feel the worst, but once they crossed the small bridge over the

Radunia Canal, and in the light of the setting sun walked into the Fish Market, full of tourists and traders, they couldn't help feeling that everyone's gaze was aimed directly at them. Fortunately it wasn't far to the small hotel on Straganiarska Street where Mr Winterhaus was staying, and in a few minutes they were there. Once they were in his room, with a view onto the leaning tower of Saint John's, Anusewicz found that he still had one coin left in his shirt pocket.

'It should be for you,' he said, handing the golden disc to Winterhaus, 'as a souvenir.'

'No, no, please keep it,' said Winterhaus, who was changing his trousers. 'I'll call a taxi for you, und this evening I am inviting you out for supper.'

'For supper?' said the brothers-in-law in amazement.

'I vill ask you to write a short statement for my vife. Saying that the money vas found, und then sank, *gut*? So she does not think I am not normal. It's enough that she thinks about my father like that.'

'May he rest in peace,' muttered Bernard, as they got into the taxi.

Anusewicz was quiet; his heart was beating irregularly, he felt breathless and wanted to be at home as soon as possible. He didn't listen to the taxi driver and Bernard's prattle when they got stuck in a traffic jam near the shipyard and the three crosses. Just as on waking that morning, some strange thoughts were bothering him again. Was Nina trying to tell him something important? Did Father Wołkonowicz appearing beside her in the meadow portend some change in his life? It was true that the day had been a mad one in every respect, but could that really have been the reason why after so many years those two had crossed deep, gloomy rivers of oblivion to appear in his dream? And what on earth could it mean – the coins of a German who had a Polish grandmother, falling into the muddy ooze at the bottom of the port river?

Under drooping eyelids, Anusewicz saw the meadows of Rudzieńszczyzna spread out along the meandering Rudejka

River, peasants raking hay, and Mr Żubrowicz, who had driven down by wagonette from Kniaziowska Góra, humming:

It's Anusewicz, there he sprawls,
The lazy old idler, scratching his balls.

It was an old, neighbourly squabble, and Anusewicz's father would customarily reply:

It's Żubrowicz, that silly old chump,
Drank away his farm and bought up a swamp.

What had originally happened and why the Anusewiczes didn't like the Żubrowiczes, he had no idea, and he knew he would never find out.

Locked away in his own thoughts, he said goodbye to Bernard and went inside the pleasantly cool flat. He drank a few sips of beer and lay down on the sofa. The Grim Reaper, left standing on his desk, gazed at Anusewicz with his immobile, glassy expression.

'Hey, old man,' he said affectionately, 'I got away from you today, you know. By a whisker, or I'd have drowned.'

And then he felt something strange. First the sofa began to spin, and with it the entire room. Once again the military band began to boom, invisible this time. The Grim Reaper jumped down to the floor, began whirling in triple time and started to grow, getting bigger by the second, and once he had reached human dimensions, he threw off his sheet-like habit. It was no longer the Grim Reaper, but Nina, aged twenty, beautiful and alluring, dancing on the carpet, as if specially for him. He wanted to go up to her, and just as in his dream, which he remembered perfectly, to touch her body. Nina began to laugh and made off into the dining room. Anusewicz went after her, but behind the wall the dining room was no longer there, just the meandering river and the meadow, the same one he remembered from his dream. On it he saw the Żubrowiczes, the Anusewiczes and all the others – those he remembered and those he had long since forgotten. Nina gave him her hand and led him towards them, but Father Wołkonowicz barred their way and told Anusewicz to look behind him. He saw his own body, which no longer belonged to him, and his wife Zofia leaning over him. She sat down on the sofa, and removed a gold coin from her husband's clenched fingers. The royal portrait did not attract her attention, but the view of the city on the reverse seemed strangely familiar. Above earthworks, forts and canals, above the tower of the Holy Virgin Mary, Saint Nicholas', Saint Catherine's and the Town Hall, above the port, the suburb and the Long Market she saw three Hebrew letters, illuminating it all from a cloud of laurel branches, blessing the city and the world. She couldn't decipher them, but guessing what they meant, she whispered that ineffable name and, holding back her tears, closed her husband's eyelids.

'Do you want to go back there?' Anusewicz heard a powerful voice, that didn't belong to Father Wołkonowicz.

'No,' he replied, 'of course not.'

And off he went, across the soft, damp meadow of Rudzieńszczyzna.

Translated from the Polish by Antonia Lloyd-Jones

Witomińska Street

ADAM KAMIŃSKI

The first time I pressed my nose to the window of the bus on the way to my new home, I went down this very street, and realised I would travel along it every day, just like the hearses carrying the deceased to the biggest cemetery in our city.

I had known Witomińska Street for ages, and it had never had any bad associations for me, though once in a while candles flickered beside its narrow roadway under the trees, and new flimsy wooden crosses replaced the old ones. Whether the car crashes there had more to do with the proximity of the cemetery than with the width of the road and the bravado of the drivers, it's hard to say. Who knows if the kingdom of death, like any other kingdom that is close to hand, doesn't tempt and entice those who can feel its force, if only for a moment?

Even in those days, near the end of primary school, I thought the street was beautiful. The trees the drivers crashed into were old, spreading chestnuts, the loveliest ones growing in the district.

In spring, when from out of nowhere white flowers appeared in the thicket of leaves on the rough, rheumatism-twisted boughs, the most delicate flowers I had ever seen, like a cascading fountain or a bird of paradise taking wing on a colour plate in an encyclopaedia, I used to come here with Tomek, to look at the local girls.

I don't know how it was that they seemed prettier, much more tempting than the ones on our street, with whom we had been playing families outside and walking to school for a good few years. You could just as easily appraise the blondes, brunettes and redheads among them, the ones with plaits and fringes, the thin and the fat, the tall and the small, and we weren't at all sure if they *were* that much prettier than our local girls. So maybe it was just their otherness, their greater distance from the girls on our street, the three or four kilometres that separated them from the places where we ate and slept, that gave them some unfamiliar, almost exotic charm. Their faces were wreathed in halos of unfamiliarity and mystery, like the head of the angel in the sculpture at the cemetery gates. But no, it wasn't just about that. I'm sure they seemed all the more charming because of the danger we exposed ourselves to by gazing after them; because their male pals spent their time sitting on the low walls too, boys who might even have exercised the right to give us a thrashing at any moment, and we couldn't have held it against them. After all, they were on their home patch. For us it was *terra incognita*, which we were viewing with the wide-open eyes of little children who have torn free of their mothers' hands at a crowded market; unfamiliar ground, fascinating and terrifying all at once.

The houses were shared by several families; they grew naturally on either side of the forest that surrounded the street, and were similar to many dotted about our district. The closer they were to the cemetery, the more they had transformed their front yards and ground floors into cramped funeral parlours, florists' bursting with muted greenery, kiosks lit up inside by lanterns, glazed galleries of carpentry workshops and multi-storey, cascading superstructures for stonemasons, on whose roofs cats would play next to the small turrets of cranes. In the driveways servile transit vans sat waiting, stripped by their owners of their frames and canvas, revealing cold, flat platforms with dimensions that recalled the proportions of the human body, as laid out in a drawing by Leonardo da Vinci. In other places luxury Mercedes Benzes were gathered – blackened and deprived of their innards, ready at any moment to receive into their empty bellies the inconceivable mystery of humanity – whose appearance outside a house other than one of these caused a violent pulse rate, and on a street other than this one bore the question, empty or full? And if full, then who might be inside? Thus they fulfilled the function of a liaison officer, an emissary of death, her envoy. It seemed as if the nearer you were to the gates into the world of the dead, the more crowded the street became, the more objects and their owners there were: flower growers, roadside salesmen, petty craftsmen and gravediggers. And yet whenever there were no cars driving down the street, perfect silence reigned here.

We ventured into the area closest to the cemetery more often in autumn than in summer, when the old chestnut trees let go of their bulbous fruits, and we went after them with our eyes on the pavement, because nowhere in the district were the chestnuts as fine and handsome as here. There they lay, without stirring anybody's interest or envy, which we found strange, because the one small chestnut tree growing by the bank at the edge of the woods in the Forest Allotments, which bore meagre, misshapen fruits, was treated as all but sacred; in autumn the backyard high priests placed a guard of honour beside it, whose aim was to grab everything that fell from it as quickly as possible. So possessing one or two fruits from this tree could be a reason for pride. We were too old by then to construct little chestnut men on matchstick scaffolding, and I cannot remember if there was some practical aim motivating us to collect them. Maybe it was enough for us that they were so pretty – in a different way from the coloured beer cans and empty Kodak, Konica and Fuji film cases brought by sailors, which performed the role of a legitimate currency at school, or the swappable parts of a collection – but pretty like shells or thunderbolts. One way or another, in the chestnut falling season, until I had stuffed my pockets full I could not walk down that street without being bent double. Only when nudged by Tomek, wanting to show off some particularly beautiful specimen, would I tear my eyes from the ground and notice that we had come almost all the way down to the gates, into the area with the florists' shops, marble gravestone galleries and front windows like the vehicle showrooms on the edges of town, though not featuring motorbikes or cars, but coffins. Wooden crosses with empty nameplates stood out on display, waiting patiently for their owners, to whom they were certainly already assigned.

Here you might see a stonemason finishing some part of a monument, a carpenter nailing a board, or a gardener bustling about in a small greenhouse. But when you took a closer look at them, you noticed that their work was not like any other, that it was being done with a special sort of concentration and detachment, in another reality, an atmosphere that drifted here from the graves, and to which their customers already belonged. They looked like shadows that the slightest wind could blow away, or that the mist could dissolve. I would watch them intently, until they vanished somewhere among the storerooms in the stratified buildings.

And then, deprived of the object of my contemplation, I would think about a girl I once saw here, before she too vanished, and I'd realise the shocking truth, that these beautiful sirens of our senses, these walking divinities of our imagination belonged to that same world. At the thought that every one of those especially appealing girls might be, if not the daughter, then the granddaughter, the niece, goddaughter or at least the neighbour of a gravedigger, the owner of a funeral parlour, a carpenter, a stonemason or the local gardener – that she might live in a house where rites were performed, a small temple of death – I felt the shudder of an important discovery and of fear go through me. Yes, their mysteriousness, remoteness and otherness were not just to do with the distance between our streets on the map of our town, but with something far more important, with a sort of vague and inconceivable difference in our actual selves.

While Tomek was organising his pockets, sorting the

chestnuts according to size and beauty, I kept thinking about what it was that fascinated and attracted us so much more than an unfamiliar shade of the skin or an unintelligible language, about the indeterminate, unnamed otherness that lay at the heart of our quest and was at the same time its aim. Without realising it, in this street we had discovered a new land, a country to fit our needs and dreams, a world that was waiting for each of us.

But we didn't want to stay there. I don't know what Tomek felt, but after stuffing his pockets he would turn and drag me back after him. I'd keep looking to left and right, swinging around and examining everything that seemed interesting and different, inhaling the odours that floated from the forest, filtered through the front yards and the graves, and listening closely to the sounds. I tried to infiltrate the landscape and to soak it in, the way the ancient haiku masters taught. But I never thought of staying there.

Taking the safest short cuts we would go home, to arrange our booty in rows in the shade of Tomek's or my home, arousing the universal admiration of our male and female friends. They would pick them up and examine them in the sunlight, like pieces of amber, trying to define the various shades of colour and weighing them in their palms, nodding their heads all the while. Someone always had a chestnut from our street's little tree on him: when he put it next to these ones, he caused general delight. When asked where the sacred groves grew, where these special fruits were from, Tomek and I replied with a unified silence. It was a secret.

One day, at the end of our walk something happened that made me wonder even more about the strangeness of this place. We didn't usually enter the cemetery, because we had no reason to, but around All Saints, when things were already getting colourful and festive, I recruited Tomek to walk down at least part of its main avenue.

It was early afternoon, and it wasn't even dusk yet. We

passed the cemetery chapel with its wooden belltower and gate, and walked along a row of small children's graves. I wasn't inspecting them all that closely, but a familiar name jumped out at me. I stopped, and Tomek came alongside me. We were standing before the little grave of Adam Kami ski, born 14 October 1978. My grave.

'Can you see what I can?' I asked Tomek.

'Yes,' he replied.

It was early afternoon, the pre-holiday rush hour. Small groups of laden people were making their way inside the cemetery, and those freed of their burdens were coming back down to the gates. I joined the latter, though I was bearing more now than on the way here. I couldn't believe what I had seen. I was shocked. I was crying. Tomek came after me.

A few days later, once I had calmed down, we went back to the cemetery. I wanted to look at it once more, to stand face to face with it again. But although we examined each of the children's gravestones several times over, there was no trace of the one that belonged to me. I couldn't understand it, but I felt relief. It was better like that, even if I had failed to explain the earlier incident. If I hadn't had a witness, I might have regarded it as a hallucination, a waking dream, an illusion that could happen to anyone.

In any case, to this day I don't know what happened then – I don't know and I no longer wonder about it. The bus stops at the head of the street, where it picks up the widows and widowers with fresh flowers in one hand and bags containing small rakes and brooms in the other. It sets them down at the other stop, right by the cemetery. Witomińska Street looks just as it did many years ago, though neither Tomek nor I come here to look at the girls or collect chestnuts now. The cemetery is there, just as it always was, filling people with the hope that something will survive after them. Only the fence has been replaced with a new one.

Translated from the Polish by Antonia Lloyd-Jones

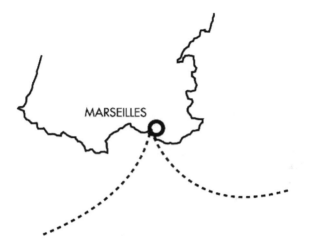

The End of the Quays

JEAN-CLAUDE IZZO

For Marie-Hélène

The Quays were Gérard's life. Where he'd always lived. Quai de la Joliette, above the Bar de l'Espérance. Where he'd always worked, too. Like his Dad. In the docks.

In the docks. Gérard didn't care to remember those years. Not tonight. Tonight it was too late. He knew that. Though he didn't know how he had come to hit rock-bottom like this, bite the dust. It had made Gérard smile when he heard Vigouroux, who used to be mayor, declare: 'In spite of the social reorganization I don't know anyone in the docks who's been reduced to begging.' That was four years ago, and it was true then. Now Gérard did know someone. Himself.

Well, okay, he didn't beg like all those youngsters he saw in the underground outside the post office; he still had enough to get himself something to eat, and drink a pastis or two in Jeannot's café.

'Hey, you listening to me?'

'For God's sake Jeannot! Why the fuck should I care about the new Alfa Romeo? Neither you nor me can afford cars like that.'

'Shit, it doesn't hurt to talk about it, does it?'

'Give us a drink!'

He ought to go home and sleep. He had had enough to get him to sleep. More than enough this evening. He looked at the clock. Ten past ten. He'd been there for two hours.

'Ten o'clock already,' he said wearily.

'Why, you got a date?' Jeannot laughed.

'You bastard!'

He had had plenty of dates. When he was still getting a proper wage. He was making fifteen thousand. A fair whack. Women fell into his arms. He took them to Larrieu's place, at l'Estaque. Or to Fonfon's when he really wanted to impress. Peroxide blondes, preferably. Fonfon's at the Vallon des Aufes went down a treat with the opposite sex. They were all dying to get their feet under the table there. He finished them off afterwards at the Son des Guitares, Place de l'Opéra. Baby and Baby, the works.

The good life.

'I was making fifteen thousand. Imagine that!'

'I never managed that much. Ten at the most. And I started work same time as you.'

'Are you kidding! Behind the bar… You don't know what work is. The port…'

'I know that's different. And not for me, thank you very much. Just the same, all this time… Now, I'm happy if I make six thousand.'

'Tomorrow, the way things are going, you'll be shutting up shop. And you won't be happy then, Jeannot.'

'Don't talk shit! It's going to be swarming with tourists here. Not the darkies, no, the ones with the dosh. Germans, Americans, Japanese…'

The modern dream. Revamping the port. Luxury cruises calling in at Marseille. Yep, that's all people talked about. We'd have a huge tourist port. A new marina at l'Estaque. What was it they called it, at the town hall? Revitalisation. Gérard had read it in the papers last year. Everyone had. Well, to be honest, with all the pastis he'd got down him, he didn't remember anything very much. But he did remember that among all the measures proposed there was not a single one that took account of the dockers.

All that lot cared about was developing businesses, the politics of who owned what land, key areas, tourism and commerce. And communication. Yep, you had to communicate if you wanted to get anywhere. Gérard thought it was daft. Paying people to talk about other people's work.

'People aren't interested in work...'

'What?'

'Hey, and you're telling me I don't listen!'

'Yeah, I know, but there isn't any work any more. So...'

'And I'm saying that where there is work you have to safeguard it and that's that. Can't argue! Like Gilbert says, when we arrived, there was a place for us. Well, it has to be the same for the ones coming on now.'

Dockers. Yes, they had struggled. For their work. And for the port. In the face of total scepticism. Not to mention general indifference.

What mattered most these last few years were the opinions of the top brass in the town. Those who had the right to speak on the telly and in the papers. The port's dying, same old story again and again. They made a best-seller out of it. Sold as many as the OM-Valenciennes magazine! And the blame was always laid on them, the dockers. 'You'd be mad to kill the goose that lays the golden egg. And all because of a thousand or fifteen hundred.' The dockers.

When Gérard was young, when he had clocked in for the first time at 5.30 in the morning, the dockers were the town's future. Today, outside the area of la Joliette, when he said the word 'docker' he could practically hear people thinking 'gravedigger'. Between 82 and 87 social planning had got rid of four hundred. Then there had been the 'disaster' of 92. It was the old ones they sacked. The ones who knew their job. Like he did.

One day nobody needed Gérard any more. After fifteen years at Intramar, as timekeeper. Not flexible enough, that's what they told him at the packing company. Not flexible enough. Scum of the earth. Port gravedigger.

'Not like it used to be,' said Jeannot, for something to say.

And he poured another round of pastis. Like Lulu said, before she pushed off:

'You'll end up drinking the whole bar!' 'Yeah,' he had replied to Lulu. 'Well, better for me to drink it than the taxes!'

'Like it used to be, for God's sake! You didn't used to have a bridge with those bloody cars up above your head. Shit!'

Gérard's windows looked out onto the bridge. When he opened his shutters he couldn't breathe for cars. Not that he'd opened them in ages. And he couldn't give a shit now in any case. Tomorrow, or the day after, the bailiffs would come and chuck him out. Gérard would be on the street. He hadn't paid his rent for months. Well shit, why should I pay for a room where I can't even open the shutters! He had told himself that one night. Since then he had boozed away his rent. Beer, pastis, rosé, beer, pastis, rosé. Twice a day. Like before, when he'd been hired. Except that he'd changed his hours. And it wasn't 5.30 and 12.30 any more, it was 10.30 and 6.30. Beer, pastis, rosé. Beer, pastis, rosé.

'You think they'll take the footbridge away?'

'Everything... they'll take everything away. The bridge, the J3, the J4[1], the Arabs, you, the bar... One day you'll wake up and find it's not your place any more. It'll be like Nice, only bigger, and even more stupid! And what's more you'll have a mayor from the National Front into the bargain.'

Jeannot grew thoughtful. He couldn't conceive of that. He just couldn't. And suddenly the pastis turned in his imagination from yellow to grey.

'Yeah,' he said sadly.

'What do you mean, 'yeah'?'

---

1. The old J3 and J4 piers were at the heart of the new developments on the Marseille waterfront.

'You better go home, Gérard. Reckon I'll close now.'

Out in the street, Gérard lit a cigarette and took a few unsteady steps, until he reached the door to his block of flats. He heard Jeannot's metal shutters coming down. Like the blade of a guillotine. On their lives, his and Jeannot's. But Jeannot didn't realize all that. He lived in hope, Jeannot did. Always had. Even when Lulu scarpered and took the little girl with her, Jeannot didn't put his head in a bucket. Life goes on, he said. But then Jeannot had the bar. He, Gérard, had nothing. Not even the memory of an unfaithful wife.

He sat down heavily on the step outside the door to smoke his fag. To think about things. It had all been going round in his head too long. And each time he saw some way out of his problems the guillotine fell. Like Jeannot's metal shutters.

Last night he had made up his mind to go and see Gilbert at the union. He might help him, give him some advice, anything, just a word, so that he could listen to something apart from Jeannot's fatuous remarks. And his own. The ones he came out with all the time he was drinking his pastis. The ones he rehearsed in his dirty shithole of a room. The worst. It was because of that, because of all those useless ideas, that he had wanted to have a word with Gilbert. Not because of the bailiffs, no. Once you've had the CRS[2] on your back you aren't scared of the bailiffs. He would deal with that. He still had a little bit of money so those gits would give him a while longer. A little while. And anyway, shit, if it didn't work out, he would go and sleep at Jeannot's. In the bar. In any case he never slept a wink at night. His worries. The cars. Even after twenty glasses of pastis and two bottles of rosé he still couldn't sleep. God knows, he'd tried.

2. Compagnies Républicaines de Sécurité (French riot police).

He got up. He hadn't gone to see Gilbert. No point, he told himself. He was only a wino now. What could you say to a wino? And besides, he hadn't set foot in the union for ages. Not since the 93 strike. Ages ago. So what was the point of marking time in Gilbert's office?

He crossed the road and climbed calmly back to la Joliette station. At the access point he waved a little greeting to the man on duty. And he went into the port. His home. They were getting to know Gérard. He often came wandering along the wharves of an evening or at night. Especially in summer. He didn't like sleeping with the window shut. And when the windows were open it was as if the cars came in through one ear and out the other.

Gérard walked along the quays. Without glancing once at the ferries. He only had one thought in his head, to go as far as J4. On the way he ascertained that the inside of the J3 shed was now entirely demolished. They'll dynamite it soon, he thought. It would be J4 next. Marseille was turning the page on the glory days of the big transatlantic companies. What would they do at the top afterwards? He hadn't the least idea. They would make money, that was for sure. Everybody was lining their pockets. The designers, the promoters, the constructors, the communicators...

But perhaps they would open up the port to the people who lived in Marseille. At last. He smiled a little at that thought. It was everyone's dream... The old, the very young. They had done a survey. 94% of people wanted the sea-front opened up. The current mayor had committed himself to it before the city council. 'So long as we safeguard economic activity,' he added. Of course. Safeguard it against people who always want too much, who talk too much, who dream too much. As if we were pigs, able to swallow any damn thing.

'We're not pigs!' he bellowed into the darkness. That made him laugh. In any case, opening up the sea-front was the pill to make us swallow all the rest. Everything they rammed down our throats. The plans were there, all ready in their little cardboard boxes. He had read that again in the papers this morning. They had pacified the port. Next they would pacify Marseille. They would finish putting the colour on the blocks of flats and the houses, and the deed would be done. Marseille would be beautiful, clean, renovated.

Another town. Another life.

He sat down on the end of the quay. His feet dangled over the water. The dark grey outline of J4 rose behind him. The last ghost of the town. Gérard wasn't nostalgic. Only sad. And tired. The town's dreams no longer bore any relation to his own. For the first time he felt like a stranger in his own home. In the docks. And therefore in his life.

After drawing on it at length and burning his fingers, he threw his cigarette into the water. It was a lovely autumn night, for God's sake. The smell coming up from the sea was the nicest smell he knew. And it was especially good this evening. A gull flew screaming overhead.

Gérard dived. He couldn't swim. He'd never learnt.

Translated from the French by Helen Constantine

The Cave and the Footbridge

CHRISTIAN GARCIN

I taught for years in a school in a district in the north of Marseille. To get there I had to take the Autoroute Est, then the Prado-Carénage tunnel that crosses part of the town, and then the tunnel that drops down under the Vieux Port before veering off north. After that I had to make my way round the cathedral of La Major, and, when I drew level with the Quai de la Joliette, join the Autoroute du Littoral, eventually coming out by Saint Henri, between the conurbation of La Castellane, where Zinédine Zidane grew up, and one of the biggest commercial centres in this area. Amazing – as a Year 10 pupil of mine, not the brightest, but among the most articulate, once observed – that they should put the centre there where folk lived who couldn't afford all the things on abundant offer to them every day. She told me she had realized that day the meaning of the word 'enslavement'.

At the start of the Autoroute du Littoral was a footbridge under which there was a kind of concrete no man's land, adjoining warehouses and rows of containers. In a film by Robert Guédiguian – I can't remember which, perhaps *La Ville est Tranquille* – it was turned into a place for prostitutes. All the years I taught in this school in the north of Marseille and passed the bridge over the Autoroute du Littoral, no matter what time it happened to be, in whatever season and whatever the weather, I would see a man sitting each day against the wall or on the pavement, staring fixedly at the entrance to a food depot ('Asia Food Market' or ' Wholesale Goods Storage') situated on the other side of the footbridge.

This man was very tall, with a dark skin, and he hardly moved. His stare, at once fixed and slightly unseeing, never swerved from this entrance. I never saw him in the evening when I passed the same place. Yet every morning, winter or summer, come rain or shine, bitter wind or blazing sun, there he was, sometimes with a hat of sorts on his head, his eyes riveted on the entrance to the goods depot. His constant presence, his unchanging posture, his obsessive stare, led me to suppose that he never had any reason to leave this area and at night must have found shelter nearby – perhaps even under a footbridge over the autoroute, like the character I subsequently saw in *Mischka*, a beautiful film by Jean-François Stévenin, in the din of cars and throbbing concrete – though to do so, he must have been quite deaf. I reflected that this enigmatic character might figure in a novel or a story that I had not yet written. I also thought I would be able to make a connection between him and another character whom I had never seen but whom I knew, let's say, by reputation, and whose living quarters also intersected my journey in the mornings, a few minutes and a few hundred metres back.

Indeed there was (and still is) at the junction between the entrance and exit of the Prado tunnel a sort of concrete triangle on which I had one day seen a pile of blankets. The place is subjected to a constant flow of traffic, stink and black smoke, and getting into it, moreover, is particularly fraught with difficulties, so it was impossible to imagine that anyone could have a dwelling there, even on the odd occasion. I suppose the blankets had all been put or thrown there for some other reason I was unaware of. Perhaps they belonged to the man who was known as The Hermit, who several years before had made a camp twenty metres above that place in a fissure in the calcareous rock which towers over the entrance and exit to this tunnel, just below the Fort Saint-Nicolas. Although I never saw the man, his dwelling-place, if you looked for it, was perfectly easy to make out in the sheer white rock face: shreds of cloth waved around there in the wind, a little like the *lung-ta*, those 'horses of the wind' of the *stupas* and other Buddhist temples you see in the Himalayas. Every morning, when I drove out of this tunnel and was about to go down into the one that runs under the Vieux Port, I looked up and saw the 'horses of the wind,' which indicated his presence, bathed in the rosy light of the rising sun, and I couldn't help reflecting that he enjoyed an unparalleled view of the Fort Saint-Jean, the town hall, the Vieux Port and the tall masts of hundreds of boats massed together.

After I'd finished teaching in that school, and was no longer travelling this route, I often wondered what had become of the tall Comorian[3] (as he was in my imagination) on the Autoroute du Littoral. One morning I decided to try and find out. I went there, taking the same road, the Autoroute Est, the Prado-Carénage tunnel, the tunnel under the Vieux Port, but I could not get to the bridge that permitted access to the Autoroute du Littoral: access was now via another tunnel, which I had never been in, and which, after the extension of the tunnel of the Vieux Port, went under the cathedral of La Major. I took the first possible exit, went back again, drove hundreds of metres along obscure roads near the sea, got rather lost, and finally reached the place where I used to see him, or so I thought. But everything had changed: the wall he had propped up so stoically and mysteriously every day had vanished, as had the pavement on which, in the film, the prostitutes stopped the cars. The whole district had been drastically altered as a result of a succession of road-works, before the opening of the second half of the tunnel which ran under the cathedral, and after the more comprehensive revitalization of the entire area, which was intended to become something of a shop window, with offices, boutiques and the usual shops and businesses. I don't know what became of this

3. A native of the Comoros Islands, once a French colony, situated in the Indian Ocean to the north-west of Madagascar.

man. I know nothing about the other one either, the 'hermit' that I never set eyes on, and I have no idea if he is still in his little cave under the Saint-Nicolas fort. But I do know that the 'horses in the wind' obstinately carry on blowing up there.

During the years I took the Prado-Carénage tunnel and the Autoroute du Littoral, I told myself that sometime in the future I would write a story or novel about these two characters who were very much on my mind. At that time I did not know where, when or how, but I knew they would be in it. When I began writing my novel *L'Embarquement* I quickly worked them into the story. Thus in this novel I was able to mix two characters who, to acquire life on paper, were based not on these two men, but on the idea that I had formed of them. They established themselves in a completely natural way, found their place immediately, took possession of the fictional space I reserved for them. One spends his days at the entrance to a depot waiting for imaginary beautiful women who, he says, still wave at him from their vanished windows; the other is an ex-legionnaire, stone-deaf, who lives in the concrete triangle that separates the entrances and exits of the Prado tunnel. Both play an important part in the life of the main character, Thomas. I must say that right at the beginning I had a few scruples: in fact I had the unpleasant feeling that I was illegitimately appropriating their real lives, as complex as they are irreducible, in the service of a dubious literary project. But then, as the characters they had inspired on paper gradually took on their own life and place in the fictional space I had ascribed to them, I became certain in the end that all I was doing was paying tribute to these two mysterious individuals, who, unknown to them, had been on my mind for so long.

The following is an extract from Christian Garcin's novel L'Embarquement.

When I met Thomas, he reminded me of a photo I had seen a little while before in the papers, of one of those tramps nobody ever talks about who are much in evidence in certain suburbs in Japanese towns, and of whom I myself saw several examples when I went to the district of Sanya in Tokyo, and in Kamagasaki in the south of Osaka. Men who were completely destitute, SDFs[4], as they are called in our euphemistic parlance so fond of all sorts of acronyms and abbreviations. When I was a child, we called them 'cloches' or 'clochards'. Over there they also call them *furosha*, the men of the wave. In the States they are *homeguards*. They are former blue- or white-collar workers who used to live a normal life, with a job, family, house, but who have gone off the rails, been cast aside and forgotten in the ebb and flow of the tide of liberalism – the violent, indifferent, pitiless liberal wave. Thomas himself had a home worthy of the name, and even had savings, not much perhaps, since he did not do a lot of work, but enough; a sister and two nephews whom he saw and still does see quite regularly; a computer, a car, and so on. But it was more his physical aspect that reminded me of the photo: thickset, bent, sullen, with yesterday's stubble and permanently surrounded by a cloud of smoke, cigars or cigarettes, depending on the time of day; not very talkative, his tatty old raincoat hastily flung on, an air of having seen it all before. He had just had an unhappy affair with a woman called Paola de Bologna, if I remember rightly, who had 'dropped him like a piece of shit', his exact words. I could never find out any more than that. He was going through a bad patch, not writing a word, drinking like a fish, keeping company with big-hearted junkies, he said. One was called André or Dédé (I don't know why so many

4. Sans Domicile Fixe (Of No Fixed Abode)

tramps are called Dédé); a former legionnaire, he was one-armed and stone deaf – something about a bomb exploding too near him somewhere in Africa – fifty years old, looked seventy, and bedded down at the entrance to the Prado-Carénage tunnel, in a sort of triangle between the entrance and the exit, where he had erected a makeshift cardboard shelter under a concrete canopy out of sight of prying eyes. In that place, of course, the traffic never stops, but as I mentioned, he was deaf. Then there was Mouloud, a huge and slightly tipsy Comorian who spent his days under the bridge over the Autoroute du Littoral, staring at a window where he had once caught sight of a pretty girl waving at him, or at least that was what he said. Thomas had grown fond of them, friendly with them. I don't think it was out of pity, though no doubt there was some compassion in there somewhere, but mainly it was a secret complicity, as you might say – the sudden revelation of a closeness, his possibly unhealthy attraction to a life that he was incapable of living himself, but which he could sometimes subscribe to, so convinced was he of the pointlessness in planning or doing anything, or of having any kind of hope there might be what you could call meaning in our existence. Months later he told me that on balance, Dédé and Mouloud were the people he felt closest to, or anyway much much closer to than others he had rubbed shoulders with, especially in the jobs he had had, who all seemed to him to be acting in a more or less meaningless way according to codes deriving straight out of the artificial world of the media, repeating the things they heard there, appropriating opinions not their own. Even if Dédé and Mouloud after their fashion were just as predictable in their ideas and opinions, they avoided the general parroting. It was undoubtedly this, as well as their human qualities, and the closeness he detected between them and him that had attracted Thomas.

Translated from the French by Helen Constantine

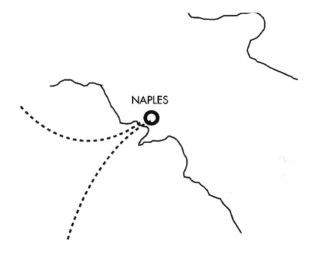

NAPLES

Right in the Eyes

VALERIA PARRELLA

I'd always liked the Cripple. He called me *Guapetella*[5] because I gave him a hard time. Even after I'd decided I was going to be his woman, I made sure I kept him hanging on. I didn't want him to think he'd got it easy.

His wife respected me, I respected her. After all, the only thing she really wanted was him to bring home his pay packet from the railways and make himself scarce in the evenings.

That was all there was to it. We had nothing else to do with each other. The Cripple ate at mine, I washed his work clothes. Once he'd left his monthly pay cheque with his wife and kids, the Cripple spent the rest of what he made with me.

We had a great time. If he'd been lucky enough to land a big job the Cripple made as much as five million in a day, or even a Rolex, or a stereo: he never came home with his hands empty. We went to Pozzuoli and splashed out on fish suppers.

The Cripple and the *Guapetella*.

'You could do better...' But I genuinely liked the Cripple.

I remember when I went to school in the mornings, I'd stop off to say hello to my mum who was standing round the little fire with the other women who were selling illegal cigs. I'd hang around, warming myself up, until I saw him appear at

5. Invented feminine form of the word for 'leader' or the 'boss'.

the top of the street, dragging his right leg behind him.

I was in the third year of training to be a nursery nurse. When I got the diploma I'd be done with school. I was sixteen and had a body that made even the priests' heads turn.

A few teachers tried it on with me, but I wasn't interested in men: I looked at women. We shared the school building with other institutes, and I always watched the girls from the sixth form college. They were light, slim and had small breasts and bobbed hair. They never tried to dodge paying on the bus.

On parents' evening, one of my schoolfriends' aunts came with all of us from the neighbourhood and took the reports for everyone. It wasn't right but the teacher wouldn't complain: each one of us weighed at least twenty kilos more than she did.

I sat there and studied the mothers of those other girls. They were *signore*, elegant women accompanied by husbands, with low heels and little make up. The teachers and the headmaster were always bursting with compliments.

'She's got money,' said the aunt.

She certainly did, but so did we: there was no shortage of money in our neighbourhood, but still you never heard anyone whisper *signora* like that, enunciating all the syllables.

We left school with our three-year diploma because our neighbourhood was tough, and more than that, it was changing: you only had enough time to make money and then you had to make more. TV antennas sprung up from the medieval loggias. On Supportico Lopez, which hadn't changed since the Spanish had built it, a tanning centre opened. *Yellow Hell*, it was called.

I never used a lamp, the women who I wanted to become had perfect golden skin, and put sun cream on when they went to the beach. They weren't like us. We were only happy if we got so red we couldn't put our bras on.

When I was seventeen one of my schoolmates had a kid in the Ruesh clinic: you couldn't have kids unless you had them there, you couldn't have all the visitors from the neighbourhood if the room didn't cost at least six hundred thousand a night. The kid weighed four kilos and to get it out they had to tear her apart. My friend was breast feeding with fifteen stitches, and when she put it to her nipple it made her cry.

'She's a nasty little bitch.'

'No,' said the doctor. 'She's not nasty. It's life: life will do anything to survive.'

That evening I went home and got together with the Cripple.

I really did like him, but I took more from him than I gave. That was the price he'd have to pay if he wanted to be with a seventeen year-old, him being thirty-five. I didn't have a dad, and anyway, no one in the neighbourhood was too bothered about that stuff.

The Cripple's wife lived at the top of the street and never went out, not like me. Everyone knew me, and everyone called me *Guapetella*, just like he did.

If I'd been the daughter I wanted to be, of the woman I wanted to become, then my mother would have reported the Cripple and sent me abroad to study. But my mother just said:

'Make sure he gets you a place to live.'

I'd already thought about it: for my eighteenth birthday present the Cripple had signed over a flat to me.

'Let's fill it full of blacks, that way you'll have a nice little monthly income.'

Everybody put blacks in their apartments.

'No. I want to put students in it. They'll keep it cleaner and pay loads more.'

Even the ones from out of town, 80 square metres, you could fit loads of them in.

In the summer, the Cripple gave me a hundred thousand every

day so I could go to the beach in Baia with my sisters. He popped into work to show his face then caught up with us later.

But one day a kid from the neighbourhood showed up on his scooter.

'The Cripple sent me. They got him in the chest.'

The bullet had lodged a few centimetres from his lung.

A neighbourhood businessman, the Prince, had taken him to his trusty doctor, a guy who had a little room near the old hospital with a few instruments, a couple of bottles of medicine, and where no one else ever went.

'He's out of danger. But without an operating room, I can't get rid of the bullet. He'll have to keep it like it is.'

The Cripple was hard, the Prince didn't want any trouble:

'I'm keeping it here.'

He left it in his chest. I kissed him, then told the kid on the scooter to go and tell the Cripple's wife.

When I thanked the Prince he turned on his heel.

'*Guappetè,* I only did it for you.'

I looked him right in the eyes, and left.

On the street outside the hospital I recognised the husband of one of those women who I wanted to become. He was with a doctor who he called *professore* and asked about the birth.

The women who I wanted to become, it seemed, didn't give birth in clinics, but in hospitals.

The Cripple went home to recover with his wife. When the people heard about the bullet in his chest, everyone in the neighbourhood started to call him Highlander. I visited him every day, and I gave him a Game Boy because he didn't think he could hack staying in bed all day doing nothing.

By the beginning of winter he was back to normal and gave me a Roberto Cavalli coat. Cavalli was our designer: his clothes cost a shitload, they were advertised in all the papers and they had those leopard prints which always passed for elegance in the neighbourhood.

But it didn't make me feel dangerous or transgressive. I felt like a slag. The women who I wanted to become wore clothes from Marella, cream-coloured.

The time had come to ditch Highlander. I did it as soon as he ended up in jail.

'I'm leaving your husband. Give me his identity card. I'll go and tell him.'

While I was on my way to forge a copy I stopped at the bar and had a coffee sent to the Prince.

The Prince. He'd been a businessman like all the others, then one day he opened a shop for wedding dresses, then another near the Museo Nazionale, then another, right opposite the cathedral.

'In this city, the only person who's got another business like mine is Barbaro.'

I'd never believed he really was someone big, but somehow he'd made loads of money and was highly respected.

His favourite shop was the one near the cathedral. I went there to thank him for the roses, and found him at the door talking to a bishop.

'Princess,' he said. 'An *aperitivo*?' I knew I had him then. 'I'll just put on my jacket.'

'Don't bother. Let's not do anything fancy.'

He came out with his jacket on, he really was a good-looking man. And there I was, walking alongside him through the city. I was nearly as tall as he was, if I turned to look at him I saw his copper-coloured goatee trying to hide behind the high white collar of his shirt.

The Prince was forty. He had a daughter nearly my age. He hadn't made it all alone, but now he was enjoying life. I could enjoy it too, but I had to be careful.

He was almost in tears when he showed me his jewel, a

yellow BMW Z23. It was beautiful, but if he'd hoped to do it just with the car then he hadn't reckoned on me. 'What a lovely colour!' I said.

He stuck even closer to me, said the sweetest things, trying to say them first in Italian, then he'd get tangled up and carried on in dialect.

I had him in my fist. Everyone knew, even his wife. She was used to being cheated on, but no one had ever been 'Princess,' not even her.

She came up to me one day in her car, a nice car.

'Listen here, are you planning to ruin me? I could be your mum.'

'And you're prepared to let yourself get ruined for so little? There's enough for both of us.'

'But I really love him.'

'Well you can tell you don't know how to keep your man. You think I'm the first?'

'He wants to leave me.'

I looked her right in the eyes. I didn't want him to leave his wife, getting him to change his life wasn't what I wanted, not forever, at least.

But he'd bought a little place in Posillipo for the two of us, and I was planning on cooking for him for a few years yet.

I was about to tell her to be patient, but then I got angry because behind her I saw a woman walking into Marella. She'd got out of a taxi.

'Not my fucking problem,' I told her, and I never saw her again.

Everything hit another level with the Prince. The neighbours were very quiet, very polite. Some of them were like us, you could tell by the gold, by the gum chewed with mouth open, or too-firmly closed: Posillipo had that effect on people like us.

Then there were the others like the notary who had sold

us the place, they were radiographers, pharmacists, commercial lawyers, and their money was worth more than ours, even if we had twice as much. Behind those smiles they exchanged there were those private members' clubs where the waiting lists were always full.

One evening we were watching a mini series and I noticed that all the women in it were exactly the women who I wanted to become. I don't know if it was that real women copied the TV or the other way round, but the women who lived in the building looked like those characters, so I forgot about following the plot and started studying.

'That one there, what's she got that's different to me?'

'You're better looking, Princess.'

'Come off it. Looking at her, what's she got that's better than me?'

'Her cellphone. Tomorrow I'll get one for you too.'

From that moment on we were watching two different films. The main character walked into a room and found a coke dealer. The Prince started to get worried.

'If I had someone with a face like that come to me, I wouldn't give her a gram. With a face like that, she'd get stopped as soon as she went out.'

I suddenly understood: they were speaking Italian. Everyone in the whole film only spoke in Italian: no big words, mind, but so naturally and without effort, that I'd understood without even noticing. If there were one or two jokes in dialect, they were made by a waiter or a mechanic, just to make the posh people laugh.

The next day I went to see the students. I was only a bit older than them, but looked like their mum. I had a little chat with the one who'd been there the longest, the one who still only gave me two hundred thousand for her shared room, a kind of protected rent.

We got ourselves organised. I enrolled in a private school. In two years' time I'd finish everything and get a diploma, the girl didn't have to pay rent anymore if she gave me lessons.

Twenty-three is still a good age to change the way you talk.

The girls said I needed to read a lot, so a first-year lent me some best-sellers, the first was that one by Susanna Tamaro.

I thought it was a ridiculous book: if I'd followed my heart I'd have ended up in the back of Totonno from the scrapyard's van, pregnant at the age of thirteen.

'*Principessa, si je capess' addò vvuò arrivà, je t'aiutass.*'

'Say it in Italian.'

'If I'd of known where you're going, I'd helped you.'

'All your verbs are wrong.'

'I'm telling you that you're the princess, like. You know what I mean. I'm gonna open up a shop for you. D'you want a shop?'

'It's gotta be clean though, all kosher, like.'

'We'll call it "The Princess of Naples."'

'I want a Marella franchise, and I get to run everything, suppliers, accounts, the lot.'

'But if it's a franchise you can't put your own man in charge.'

I opened it in a strategic position, just on the edge of the neighbourhood but on the other side of the road, on the corner of the proper shopping street. I had two big windows at ground level and one on the first floor. That was where I sat.

They came down from Milan, piled up with stuff to sell. Everything had a logo on it. I greeted everyone with a smile that didn't show my teeth. I let them choose the assistants on just one condition: they weren't allowed to be from my neighbourhood.

It was useless to risk paying them under the table: in Milan it was enough to call it 'work experience'. I did everything by the book.

We only stocked sizes 38 to 46, if a larger lady came in it was only to have a look at how I was doing. In the neighbourhood they dodged the question of my name and rebaptised me 'Marella.' I never let myself be seen, not around, not in the shop. I had two small CCTV cameras and watched everything through a monitor.

When the Prince came to the shop I felt embarrassed. So as not to upset anyone I made him come straight upstairs.

It was around then I started spending time with the women I'd got to know in the gym: I spent hours doing aerobics to make myself look thinner. I wanted the body of a warrior. They were all hata yoga and massages. We went out together in the afternoons to drink tea, sometimes they introduced me to their Sri Lankan babysitters and perfect little brats who addressed me politely.

'No, honey, Mrs Marella is a friend of mummy's. You can say *tu*.'

I had a gut reaction when I heard the word 'friend' – my hand shot down into my bag to touch the flick-knife the Cripple had given me.

I tried to keep home visits to a minimum: once outside of the safe zone, unexpected dramas played themselves out.

'Mummy, you're a fucking whore,' yelled the little ones, with perfect diction.

The older snot-nosers stayed locked in their rooms, having taken the phone hostage.

One day a girl who looked as if she'd eaten nothing but crackers for weeks asked me if I was her dad's new girlfriend. I slapped her so hard I heard her bones hit the parquet floor as she fell. From that moment on I became her closest friend, and for months her mother was only able to communicate with her through me.

After a while I decided all this had nothing to do with me: the women who I was becoming only existed sitting outside the Gambrinus café, a flûte of prosecco in hand.

One morning the Senator's wife showed up at the shop. She

wanted to buy a coat.

I'd known her for ages, I remembered her electoral round-ups in the neighbourhood. She was called Anna, like my mother. For as long as I could remember, every July 26th my mother sent her a gift box from Flor-do-Cafè.

'You've changed,' she said.

I smiled at her.

'Coffee?'

But she wanted me to talk.

'Are you still with the Prince?' It was an odd question because the Senator's wife, the Senator, the Senator's last secretary and even the last paving stone of the neighbourhood all knew that we'd split up.

'No, but he sends me roses every week.' Everyone already knew this, too.

She chose a coat and asked me to deliver it, then stroked me on the cheek.

'Send my regards to your mother.'

I hated the Senator's wife for four days. Then she introduced me to the Senator.

He came just as I was closing up, with a handsome guy, younger than he was.

I sent the girls home as I was coming down the stairs, then stopped on the third stair, just to make sure I had the right appearance of power.

'Good evening,' I said, and he leant out toward my hand. I quickly pulled it away from him.

'Kisses on the hand are for priests and *mafiosi*. Who are you looking for?'

'A kiss on the hand is also for *signore*.'

'I'm not married.'

I didn't like not understanding. And anyhow, I didn't have any more weapons: I'd got rid of the Prince and his boys. The Cripple's flick-knife had become a key ring. I'd left bootleather and nail scratches behind forever. The spit of my dialect.

'I came to introduce you to the Lawyer, a close friend of mine.'

I held out my hand to him and looked him right in the eye. There was nothing else I could do.

'I do not presume to shake your hand, as it deserves so much more.'

'Please. Have a seat.'

'The Senator and I came to ask your advice, and, if possible, your help.'

They were looking for a favour. I didn't know anything about politics. I'd always voted for amnesties and pardons, just like I'd been told to.

'The elections are coming up in April.'

'Senator, you've always won the elections.'

'Yes, but the situation is different now. Not so much for the general elections, but the local ones. It's a mess: the current lot have been there for eight years.'

It took half an hour of my life to evict the students.

'Without warning?'

'Did you want a telegram?'

'Can't you at least wait until after Christmas?'

I thought about it: I needed space for the electoral committee immediately, but they weren't going to put the terracotta floor in until January anyhow. I was about to leave them with my best wishes when the bitch got cheeky:

'I lent you all those books...'

She looked at me, a bit scared, a pile of shiny books in her hand.

'OUT!' I shrieked, and threw a drawer full of knickers after her. 'ON YOUR WAY!'

The Lawyer was an out-going councillor and a protegé of the Senator. I wanted to stay clean. When he'd defended a boss he only did it because his office had to. Together we chose the furniture for a small smoking room where the men could retire to discuss the more delicate questions. It was here where the Prince poured out his contribution to the cause in grams.

At this point I could have set off fireworks every evening. I could act like a prima donna: they were my guests, they were my putative lovers.

But I decided to give it the final push.

I invited the Lawyer out to lunch and gave him the keys to my apartment. 'I think you can do better than anyone else.'

'I didn't know you could be so understated.'

'You don't know anything about me. But you can still get to find out.'

'This evening?'

'Whenever the party leaves you free time. I'm a patient woman.'

I rarely showed my face at the committee meetings, was home by eleven at the latest, always taking a taxi. All January I wore drab colours and my hair in a chignon. I took so much time to do my make up I ended up looking like I hadn't put on any make up at all. The Senator looked at me carefully: only once I caught his eye and he was looking at me like a man who has understood and approves. He had a chignon too, in his way.

The Lawyer tried to get me into bed three times. Obviously, I couldn't play at being Saint Maria Goretti for ever, so I just tried to make him think I was exceptional.

'This time it's different,' I said. 'Please excuse me.'

The fourth time I let him succeed, after dinner, my place: I'd been saving a blowjob like that for ages.

We decided to get married after the election, then I'd give him the shop to manage and the apartment to rent, while I'd just vanish and play at being the wife: his career would mean travel, regular visits to the capital. I had to make sure I was free to do all that.

The committee held a small party. Enough toasts were made to get us sufficiently drunk.

But still it seemed I hadn't done my calculations properly. Being a bit out of the picture, I'd thought that a man and a woman who were both decided was all that was necessary for a wedding. I hadn't realised that first I had to marry his friends, the family name. His mother.

His family didn't want to meet me: they'd been informed, and my past, which was my only motive, had also become my only obstacle. He was genuinely in love and the fact embarrassed him. The problem sat between us in silence. If I ever mentioned it, he just said: 'It's not important.'

But I didn't know what I had to feel so guilty about. Basically, I was supposed to be getting engaged to a thirty-five year-old cokehead who still lived with his mother.

Meanwhile, the elections were getting closer and would soon have passed. If everything went well they'd put some lead in his pencil, give him some encouragement: strong men need to feel they can manage without any help.

If I'd still been the same girl I was I'd have smelt the danger like an animal, I'd have tensed my muscles and leapt into the only course of action possible, pretending to be above it all, or disappearing.

But now I stayed up late, going through all the possible variables. I got interested in different ways of solving the problem, in doing something new and decisive to make me the woman I wanted to be.

I could have taken Smarties instead of the pill.

But I just sat and waited.

Seventy-two hours after the end of the electoral campaign I put on a pair of leather trousers and some dark glasses. I called the Senator on his mobile and fixed an appointment on the corner of the neighbourhood.

'Get in,' I said as I opened the car door. 'Let's talk.'

I turned into via Stella, Santa Maria Antesaecula, salita Capodimonte, then stopped at the old Observatory. They were streets he didn't know. He was from people who didn't know these streets.

'Get out, Senator.'

We walked for fifty metres through the long undergrowth. There were plastic bags, empty bottles, syringes under our feet. Then the city. All of it, right out as far as the sea. I thought about Totonno from the scrapyard.

'Senator, please try to understand me. Votes bought for a hundred thousand lire. Heavies outside the polling stations. Checking stamps on the ballot papers. This is what I know about politics. This is what you've given us for thirty years. Isn't that right? But maybe this time that won't be necessary. Isn't that right? And why's that?' He looked at Capri. 'Not because we've changed, Senator: it's because now we've actually created a real consensus.'

The day before the elections the Senator sent a car to pick up my mother.

'Make sure you're dressed in black,' I'd told her. 'You're a widow. And don't talk much.'

From the depths of her sixty years my mother didn't feel old or a widow, but she was intelligent and understood that it was better if she seemed so. An aged widow couldn't do anything other than say, 'We've got him round our little finger.'

I gave her a hard look: I didn't want to hear about anything wrapped around fingers right now.

My future in-laws arrived at home in rapid succession: the Senator with my mother, me and the Senator's wife, the cake from Scaturchio. My fiancé was so happy. My mother nodded and smiled at him, a little blessing. For the rest of the afternoon the Senator's wife held my mother's hand in her own.

The Senator held court for as long as was necessary for my mother-in-law to study me, then she raised her glass and made a toast.

She would take care of everything. We could sign the forms after the first round of voting and before the run-off. The Senator would be my witness, as long as the Lawyer hurried up and found one for himself.

That evening he took me home and we did it in the car, the next day they won: the Senator took Rome and my fiancé got onto the council in the first round. When we went to the town hall to sign the papers a traffic warden nodded at us reverentially. Then we had to get the party organised as the prime minister was arriving in town to support a candidate in the run-off vote. But we didn't care at this point. Walking out onto Piazza Municipio I found myself between the pines and the port terminal, Vesuvius behind us.

It was in that moment that my father-in-law offered me his arm and whispered the word: *Signora.*

Translated from the Italian by C. D. Rose

Beneath the
Torregaveta Sun

PEPPE LANZETTA

Torregaveta is rubbish. Torregaveta stinks of old mussels, shells left on the ground. The music of Level 42 can be heard from the car radio of a Fiat Panda parked with the door open. A boy enjoys the sun sitting in a bar with three shabby little tables. Torregaveta swarms with rubbish under the Monte di Procida; there's a long jetty where lads with burned skin go fishing with homemade rods, and at four o'clock in the afternoon a trawler full of mussels arrives... only mussels, for other seafood people go to Monte di Procida. Here there are only musselsmusselsmussels. Beach encrusted with paperfruitpeelscansneedlescondomsglassbottles. Dirty water, black sea. Why is the sea at Torregaveta so black?... And on windy, winter days, the sea is even blacker. But the sun always shines in Torregaveta.

And the Cumana. The old, faithful Cumana, the little old rowdy train that still transports people from Naples who come swimming here: in this seaside Bronx.

Torregaveta swarms with rubbish: dried, squeezed lemons on the ground, lemon for mussels. Cumana, how long do you stop? Because you don't leave every five minutes like a fast underground train, instead you stop: chunky, dirty, old, neglected... lazy... tiredtired... what are you doing? You leave every twenty minutes? Or every half hour?

And the children who play inside the station and even

on the trains get on at one door and get off at another... Cumana, sometimes you used to stop right by the sea, you arrived 50 metres away from the sandy shore, 50 metres from that dirtyfilthy sea... you need to be brave to jump in and swim and bathe in those waters full of tetanus and hepatitis, dermatosis and floating condoms used during the nights of fire spent dreaming of Ibiza or Formentera. Old and stinking Torregaveta, you'll never be Ibiza. You dreamed about the tourists of World Cup Italia 1990. But they didn't bring the tourists here; what is there to see anyhow? Sorry, old and mussel-filled Torregaveta. Your sea is black. You've got emaciated, scrawny children who run along your shitty shore and happily dip their little feet in the water without realising that in a different and faraway world there are the Seychelles, Maldives, Mauritius and Palma in Majorca. And Capri. Why, Torregaveta, aren't you like Capri? Why don't the VIPs flock to your shores?

TorregavetaCumaFusaroMiliscola, you all have the same smell, the same wretchedness, Torregaveta queen of nothing.

And the few people who go down to the beach in May delude themselves that they're enjoying the first bit of sun here because they'll be abroad, on a cruise or on some island in the Pacific for the second and third sunny periods... but instead they'll still be here in the suffocating heat of August, along with the others, along with those who've never moved away from here, confused and soaked, camouflaged, wearing old swimsuits and fashionable swimsuits, but still here, beneath the large rock of Monte di Procida, with their shorts and beach balls. Cursed Torregaveta, why weren't you born in Brazil? Why did you come and settle here, where there's no glory, no money and no God...

And the fried smell of fried macaroni pizzas and the stench of *parmigiana di melanzane* and the oil that drips from the pepper panini and the mortadella panini all resemble you... they're like you.

They're part of the scenery. After bathing in it so much

we think of the sea afterwards, and we piss in the sea, and we spit in the sea and there are even people who make love in those filthy waters that mingle with the sperm and what remains of an old salty tang contaminated by the sewers and drains...

Why doesn't Pavarotti come and sing on your sandy shore? Why have Pink Floyd played in Venice and not here, old Torregaveta with no monumentshistoryColiseum CathedralArchofTrajanMaschioAngioino? Why don't they build a big Sheraton hotel here?

And at night the sea crashes against the foreshore which, if it could speak, would describe all the faces, hands, feet, music cassettes, cassette players, snacks, lunches, sandwiches, onion frittatas, egg frittatas, aubergines, cockles, fried chicken, thermos flasks of coffee, winebeermineralwatercocacola it has seen... all the stories of love and squalor it has heard, all those I Love Yous, all the oaths, all those 'If you leave me, I'll kill you', all those 'If you love me, you must come and talk at my house, with my parents', all those 'I really like Tonino, look what beautiful curly hair he has. You know, Annalisa, yesterday he took me to the beach hut and showed it to me... oh my! Annalisa, what an effect it had on me, how beautiful it is, what a beautiful mouth Tonino has, Annalisa, I can't take any more, if I don't see him I feel ill, if I don't marry him, I'll kill myself, he's so handsome, Annalisa, you have to believe me: dark, tanned skin, dark curly hair, Ilovehim...'

And Pino Daniele sings: 'You need to see it through even if you've been a bit disappointed in this love affair, you feel a lil' curious...'

And Giggino hasn't been down to the beach in three days and nobody has seen him and Annalisa can't rest... She looks over and over again under his beach umbrella, she looks under his friend's beach umbrella, she looks over and over again at Giggino's window which has a view over the Tramonto bar, seen perfectly from the beach. Due to the hot weather, the window is closed, his brothers and his mum are on the beach, but Giggino isn't there… and Annalisa is so crazy-worried she doesn't even go swimming and feels too ashamed to ask around to find out what's become of Giggino…

Annalisa is stubborn as a mule; she had an argument with Giggino, she's jealous, too jealous, and Giggino has lots of young girls hanging around him but he loves Annalisa and she knows this… but she's jealous all the same… and they had an argument… and why does he now have to mull over it for so long?

And on the beach this morning Signora Bice's son found a small packet of Rohypnol and a little strip of capsules with only 2 left… Who knows who came here last night to get fucked and even forgot the packet… But Jesus Christ, how can they stuff themselves with these Rohypnol that destroy your liver, kidneys and stomach…? The doctor gave some to my sister Mariarosaria, says Signora Bice, when she wasn't right in the head… well yes, because she had a terrible nervous breakdown and couldn't sleep at all at night… But my husband told me that even junkies take these Rohypnol when they can't get hold of the real stuff… but you hear of such strange things… well I never, people leaving these drugs here, with the children on the beaches…

And what sordidness, once it was condoms, now it's Rohypnol, women's sanitary towels… what sordidness… One of these mornings, let's go to the town hall and see what must be done… this beach is already disgusting as it is… then people come here in the evening and do as they please… but why don't they employ a watchman, a security guard, someone…? At one time this really was a beautiful beach… but now… look what a bloody mess it is!!!

If my husband finds out, he won't bring us here any more…

Torregaveta, you're gradually being abandoned by everyone and who've you got left? What have you got left apart from a rusty jetty, some rotten beach huts, the Cumana train and a few mussels on the ground?

You haven't got pedaloes like in Rimini and you haven't even got any seaweed... if you had seaweed, then we'd understand why people are abandoning you... but you've got nothing, you've no algae, you've no muscular lifeguards, you've no German, Austrian, English or Swedish women... You've no nightclubs, you've no mega-discos, you've no alcoholic drinks or strong alcoholic drinks, you've no ecstasy, crack or coke... You've just got some vulgar Rohypnol and disgusting heroin... and even the heroin tastes of your sea, tastes of you, of the breeze, of the foam that blows through you when it's windy... I'd like your sea to carry away all the world's disgusting heroin and dump it in your depths, off the coast, while Capri is still sleeping, Ischia is still partying and Procida is weeping... I'd like you to sink all the shit that makes your mothers weep and your fathers despair, that kills and takes away your children... Wake up Torregaveta, put some effort in, even if you're nothing grand, put some effort in... Because when the sun comes out in May and it's not yet summer, I'll come and visit you from time to time, and even if you still don't have any chilled coffee with ice, I'll be content... All I need is a view of your jetty, a fruit juice, some children running by and I'll feel at peace...

Translated from the Italian by Helen Robertshaw

The Terminal

Murathan Mungan

As the Wings Travel bus arriving from Denizli approached the Esenler Terminal, the young attendant tried acting alert and lively while mightily fighting off sleep, and walked the aisle, serving cologne with reflex motions of his arm. Some passengers took extra squirts to rouse themselves, while others soaked their handkerchiefs to wipe the traces of sleepless travel off their faces, rubbing their necks and arms, trying to invigorate their senses.

In everyone's mouth was the night's bitter aftertaste.

Meltem had not slept much since Afyon, and kept tossing about in her seat. Taking her hand-mirror from her purse, she inspected the purple creases of sleeplessness around her eyes, their prematurely baggy underlids, yet knew she had to remain vigilant about warding off the ghosts of her past. Then again, what sort of deep sleep and how long a rest would have sufficed to restore this thoroughly exhausted face? Rather than fretting over the traces of just one night's sleeplessness – they were soft and easy to rub off – she had to get accustomed to seeing in her face the dregs of her already aging memories. She had to learn neither to worry about these nor to resist the passage of time that had a mind of its own, no matter what we did. She decided to find a fresh start in this new morning that remained cool despite the rising sun, and to enjoy the days she would share with Tamer in Istanbul.

Facing the ghosts of one's past, though vexing at times, offered one significant advantages in crossing some of life's thresholds. How she wished we could describe life not in terms of ever diminishing remains but just in terms of new beginnings.

Unhurriedly she got up from her seat, took her shoulder bag from the rack overhead, and got off the bus. On the unloading platform, the wide baggage doors on both sides of the bus were lifted open, and the passengers had gathered in front of them, waiting for their turn to pick up their suitcases.

When it was her turn, she pointed out her suitcase to the attendant.

A bus coming from Sinop had arrived at the terminal almost at the same time as hers, and was parked on the other side of the platform, adding to the crowd of passengers who were busily scanning the baggage compartments to locate their suitcases. Yıldız Hanim and her husband were standing right behind Meltem, almost shoulder to shoulder.

Even a few days' visit to Sinop had sufficed to make them miss Istanbul. While on the bus, Ma'am Yıldız had turned to her husband and said, not in a manner of asking but more like declaring, 'It wasn't this hard in the past, was it?' 'Nowadays, no matter where we travel, I am anxious to return home. Do you think we're getting old?' Her husband had smiled with calming affection and tilted his head forward.

As if they had already left behind the memories of Sinop, Seher, her house and their all too brief vacation, they wearily looked at the crowd, the harbinger of Istanbul.

In the end, everyone returned to their own life.

When Meltem and Ma'am Yıldız picked their suitcases and turned around, their eyes met. Bags in hand, each smiled understandingly and let the other pass. Ma'am Yıldız slightly bent her head and gestured a thank you. Husband and wife walked ahead and disappeared. Then, adjusting her bag on her shoulder, Meltem moved with quick steps, releasing herself from the crowd. As if moving to the beat the wobbly rollers of her suitcase made on the stone pavement, she walked toward one of the exits that opened to the parking lot where the taxi cabs were stationed.

On one of the platforms she walks by, next to the bus that is about to leave for Kırşehir, Özer is holding Tülay tightly in his arms, brushing her hair gently off her forehead, bidding her farewell with calming words and loving embraces. 'Why the teary eyes? Kırşehir is just a bus ride away. The first chance I get, I'll be there, trust me.' He gestures toward her purse, pointing to the tape he had put inside. 'Don't forget to listen,' he says, 'My voice, my heart, my songs are with you.' Most of the passengers have taken their seats in the bus, but the two want to remain in each other's arms until the very last second. One more time, Tülay buries her head in Özer's wide chest, inhales his smell. She is filled with an insuperable desire to cry. 'You will come, Özer, won't you?' she asks, her voice breaking, 'You will come, won't you?'

Meltem pulls her suitcase with its wobbly wheel, heading toward the door of the covered pass that connects the concourse to the public square; a little ahead, she hears the voice of a young woman calling out to someone, while anxiously hurrying to catch up with her, 'Sister Nihal! Sister Nihal!' Unaware that the call is intended for her, the oblivious woman is about to walk away when Meltem stops her, 'Ma'am, I think you're being called.' Curious to know to whom the voice belongs, the woman turns to look at Güzel who has been running toward her; just a couple of steps between them, Güzel slows down, looks surprised, 'Oh, I am sorry,' she says, 'I took you for someone else. Very sorry to bother you!'

She was so certain that it was Sister Nihal, and yet the woman standing before her is much younger. Meltem and the woman smile at the misunderstanding, and resume their walk.

'Ah, my foolish head,' says Güzel, bringing her hand to her forehead; her palm closes upon her forehead with an audible 'thup.' Even she is surprised by the sudden joy that had flared inside her when she thought she saw Sister Nihal. 'As if running into her in Istanbul would have changed anything!' she thinks to herself. 'Besides, how many years is it since I last saw her?' Unexpectedly and with an inexplicable longing, she hears the sound of the Green River rushing in her ears. Her gaze is caught in the sparks of a midday sun on the surface of the currents, vivid as if real, and her face is suddenly cast in the deep purple shadows of tall mountains. A dust-like, intangible sorrow settles on her shoulders – why, on account of whom, she cannot tell – as she turns around, walks back and away.

Emine, the other woman that Güzel had mistaken for her 'Sister Nihal', imagines a story around the look of surprise on the stranger's face. The person she must resemble is not just anybody for this young woman – it's obvious from the deep disappointment Emine could read in her face when she recognized her mistake. How I wish that for just a moment, by some movie trick, I were the person that she was looking for; how she stared at me, like an orphan child. If only I were able to make her happy. In a flash of recognition – akin to the sudden sting of a finger cut – Emine realizes that she no longer has anyone in her life who would run to her with such anxious anticipation, that her fancy's trigger is not the young woman but her own disappointment. Standing in the middle of the crowded bus terminal, she discovers once again the solitude that has been her companion for years.

Next to one of the main exits, a woman with a headscarf and hands folded over her belly is standing between two immense suitcases that almost block the way. As she is about to walk past her, Emine momentarily steps out of her thoughts and pauses, her attention drawn not to the suitcases but to the woman's face, the deep blue of her eyes. She can clearly read in this face the tense apprehension of waiting for someone much delayed. Even if the delay hasn't been too long, the time she has spent waiting must feel so to her. Despite the sharp outlines of her face, she scans her surroundings with the insecurity of a lost child. It's obvious that she was instructed to guard the suitcases. Who would know that this was Asiye's first time in Istanbul. They had come to visit their first grandchild from their older son who had gotten married and moved to Istanbul. Now they are returning to Gümüşhane. The baby photographs tucked in her coat's inside pocket warm Asiye's bosom.

Some passengers' faces bear the vague look of hurry or the tense anticipation of travel, others suggest sorrow or weariness akin to sorrow, while the faces of travelers with provincial attire reveal the desire to return to their hometowns, to the climate, the air, the waters familiar to them. At least these are what Emine reads in those faces. In any case, this is not Istanbul; what you see in these people – their clothes, bearing, demeanor – is Turkey. You exit Istanbul when you exit the Esenler Terminal.

Lost in the stories she has been inventing about all these faces, Emine reproaches herself when she notices that she walked past the platform for her bus departing for Edirne. She abruptly turns around, without taking into account that she could easily collide with someone in this frantic crowd. She doesn't want to complain but cannot help thinking about her co-workers' senseless determination to travel by bus. Every mishap experienced along the path taken halfheartedly only serves to heighten one's displeasure. Checking her watch, she quickens her steps; her co-workers already must be in their seats.

She again sees the woman with her immense suitcases, still standing in the same spot. She also notices a man with red hair, pale skin and a friendly smile hastily approaching the woman; he must be her husband, she thinks, since the tense apprehension on her face suddenly evaporates. Emine smiles, too, as if life has regained some of its equilibrium. She decides not to complain about the Edirne trip too much.

Aslı was pleased to hear the barker outside the ticket office repeatedly shouting, 'Bus to Manisa, departing in twenty minutes!' but, once inside, she is dispirited by the long line at the ticket window. She is angry at herself for not having reserved her seat in advance. For her, worse than not finding a seat altogether would be finding one in the very back of the bus. She joins the line, mumbling to herself. She is determined to try her luck here before checking the other bus companies. She wants to travel with this company as much as she doesn't want to miss the trial in Manisa... Just then, the woman in front of her turns around and says, 'It's likely that there will be no tickets left by the time you get to the window. You can have my ticket, if you'd like.' Noticing the look of distrust on Aslı's face, the woman feels the need to explain herself, 'I just received a phone call from Ankara, I must travel there instead.' As if one more clause were needed to convince Aslı, she adds, 'for a funeral.' Aslı looks at the ticket and the seat number. 'But it's in your name,' she says. 'That shouldn't be a problem,' Nazan replies, 'they can change it.'

Handing her ticket to Aslı, Nazan leaves the line to go and get a ticket for Ankara; on the way, she thinks of her phone conversation with her lawyer, the prospect of seeing the house in Cebeci again, and the emotions the visit would stir. Ever since the phone call, memories of the past have been flashing before her eyes; now accompanying those memories is a song that begins with 'Never will I forget,' her ears always remembering it in his voice; softly murmuring the words, she disappears in the crowded terminal.

As soon as she gets off the bus, Süsen answers her cell phone. As if repeating a secret password known to the speaker, she chants a long, 'Hello—o.' 'I just got off,' she says, 'Yes, I'm back sooner than planned, my parents are staying in Sarköy a little longer. Where would I be? The Terminal. In Esenler. A terrible place! How will I get there? Don't know. Supposedly there are taxis waiting outside, I'm headed in that direction. Where are you? When I'm on the other side, shall we go down to Cadde? Goodness! Who needs rest? As if I'm coming from America. How about we meet in front of King, Goksu?

I missed Cadde. Yes, yes, not just Cadde...'

After Göksu's last comeback, Süsen darts and skips toward the taxi stop on the public square with endless rows of taxi cabs, in her hurry bumping into a few people, apologizing to some, entirely ignoring the types she doesn't like.

One of the women she whizzes by is Suna who was finally able to breath a sigh of relief once the bus from Erzurum arrived at the platform. She had not been able to sleep since learning that they would be traveling by bus. 'You know, Ma'am Zekiye is afraid of flying,' her mother had explained on the phone. 'Besides, how often does the poor woman visit Istanbul. Plus I prefer the leisurely ride, enjoy the scenery.' No sooner had Suna brought up the option of traveling by train than her mother had cut her off, 'I cannot take the stop-and-go of the Orient Express.' Suna tries to refrain from complaining. In the end, they had arrived, and that's what mattered the most. Even though they appear exhausted, she can see the glow of excitement in their eyes...

'Welcome, dearest Ma'am Zekiye, and how many years it's been since you last visited Istanbul!' Suna says, releasing herself from Ma'am Zekiye's embrace, and gesturing to her chauffeur to carry the suitcases to the car.

At the taxi stop, as Süsen is about to reach for the door handle of a taxi, she notices the insistent horn of one of the cars parked across the street, and lifting her head, she sees Irem decked in black leather and chains, leaning against the car with her arms folded over her chest. Süsen screams with excitement, 'Damn you little pigs! You tricked me!' and as she runs toward her, Göksu and others come out of the car. 'When did you arrive from Bursa?' Süsen begins to ask but Irem cuts her off: 'Never mind that. You tell us about Kayseri, the wedding! How was it?' 'How would it be? Just a wedding. The past, always the past, they talked about nothing else!' Then she shows everyone her hennaed hands, 'It didn't wash off even in the sea,' she says. To look closely, Irem removes her wide-rimmed, ostentatious glasses. 'So how long are you staying this time?' Süsen asks her. Göksu wraps his arm around Süsen's waist, pulls her toward him, and kisses her on the neck. Playing coy, Süsen shrinks away.

One of the shuttle busses that carry passengers between Taksim Square and the Esenler Terminal comes to a stop in front of the car that Süsen, Irem and their friends had just got in, and blocks the way just when they are about to leave.

Sevgi is among the passengers who get off the shuttle bus. A faraway look in her eyes, she is headed toward her bus, when a thickset and balding man accosts her, 'Excuse me, Ma'am Doctor, greetings to you,' he says, 'Do you remember me?' Slowly coming back from her reverie, Sevgi stares intently, trying to remember the man. 'You know. From Trabzon. I was a police officer. We worked on a few cases together. Of course, I gained a bit of weight while shedding quite a bit of hair.' 'Ah, of course, I remember,' Sevgi says. Pleased to be remembered, his features soften; he squeezes his daughter's hand that he has been holding tightly. His daughter looks up, thinking that he will tell her something. 'So many years since we last saw each other,' Sevgi says. 'Where are you nowadays, Ma'am Doctor?' 'In Antep.' 'Gaziantep?' 'No, simply Antep. You know: Urfa. Maraş Antep. That's how they taught us at school. I trust my teachers.' Laughing at her own words, Sevgi overcomes her lethargy. The man thinks he should laugh, too. When she begins to ask, 'And where do you work now,' Sevgi realizes that she doesn't remember his name. 'Don't even ask, very far away, Ma'am Doctor. I got sent east. Assigned to Bingöl, although now I'm the chief commissar. I am taking my kids to Kırklareli. To their grandmother.' Again squeezing his daughter's hand, he looks at his children. Thinking that she should at least pat one of them on the head, Sevgi smiles. Tour-of-duty friendships, she thinks to herself. One barely remembers them, yet the chance encounters are still pleasant. How everything quickly becomes memory.

'And you, Ma'am Doctor, where are you traveling?'

Nazan walks past them, and enters one of the ticket

offices that are lined side by side between the public square and the terminal concourses. Securing her ticket, she hurries toward the concourse gate to catch the Ankara bus that is announced to leave shortly; she passes travelers sitting in the benches, waiting.

They sit in one of the benches, a young girl and a woman, side by side. The young girl had been perched there by her brother and sister-in-law who had instructed her not to budge until they returned from the restroom. They had looked back to check on her, and flashed a friendly smile at the stranger occupying the other seat, as if asking her to keep an eye on the young girl.

'Is this your first time in Istanbul?' she asks. 'Yes, it is my first. We visited for just a few days. We have relatives here.' Several trendy magazines with glossy covers are piled on her lap. 'So, did you enjoy your stay?' 'Yes, I did.' 'Istanbul is lovely,' she says, 'Unlike anywhere else.' She speaks these words with an unfamiliar longing in her voice. 'Do you live in Istanbul?' 'No, I don't. I live in Germany. And you?' 'We're from Izmir.' Quickly warming to each other, they enjoy the small talk for a while.

They hear a barker screaming, as if speaking into a bullhorn. 'Dear Samsun passengers, your bus is about to leave. Please proceed...'

That's when Şengül stands up, and straightens the creases off her loose-fitting, long skirt, which she had worn to be comfortable while traveling. 'My bus is leaving,' she says. She starts to add, 'It's nice to meet you,' but realizes that she doesn't know the other's name. 'Nurhayat,' the young girl says while she stands up, too. 'My name is Nurhayat.' She takes the hand of this young girl with a luminous face and pure gaze; they shake hands with an intimacy that belies their brief friendship. 'Very nice to meet you, Nurhayat,' Şengül says, 'Have a safe trip home,' then gesturing toward the brother and sister-in-law coming toward them, she adds, 'And they're right on time.'

Nurhayat waves at Şengül, bidding her farewell.

Walking down the aisle in search of her seat, Zozan reproaches herself for never remembering the numbers for the seats located right over the wheels. She knows all too well from previous travels how those seats shake and jolt in some of the old model busses. When purchasing tickets, she usually makes a point to ask, 'Please, no seats over the wheels,' but this time, in her excited state, she can't even remember if she asked. She is therefore relieved when she finds her seat; placing her bag on the overhead rack, she slides into the window seat. She knows that this journey is unlike the countless arrivals and departures over the years, that she is returning home as an attorney in training, a law school graduate. The word 'home' first evokes the image of village children with scabbed cheeks. Then an indistinct ache, coupled with the pungent smell of Dersim prairies. She feels as though she has aged by several years. Restless, she doesn't know if she can bear the long road ahead. Scenes of her family celebrating her achievement, snapshots of her relatives' faces run through her imagination. It pains her to think of her brother in prison; she wants her law degree to benefit him the most. She imagines her future in Mersin, where she will relocate after her family visit to complete her legal internship and start her professional life. Her life is like a film she is eager to see after having watched the trailer. Peering through the reflection of her face on the window, she flashes a smile at the void, her eyes gleaming with joy. 'I will finish school without losing even a year, and defend life without losing even a single trial.' This is what she had promised herself when she succeeded at the entrance exams. Having fulfilled one half of her pledge, her heart renews its promise for the rest.

From the moment she gets on the bus, the woman with dark, sun-scorched skin anxiously scans the rows of seats as she walks up the aisle with an unsteady gait, holding onto the headrests on both sides; she finally comes and sits next to Zozan. A young man who looks not much older than a child, a relative who had apparently come along to see her off, takes her bag and places it on the rack above. Both of their faces bear the expression of an obviously fresh sadness. After they whisper a few words to each other and exchange doleful glances, the young man kisses the woman's hand, vaguely smiles at Zozan and gets off the bus. He stands in a spot on the platform where he can see the woman. He will obviously stay there until the bus departs, and not leave before waving a last farewell at her. Zozan and the woman staring out the window catch each other's glances a few times, exchanging smiles. Her grief covers her face like a layer of ice; each time she musters a smile, it's as though her face is breaking open.

As the paths, the stories, at times the destinies, of countless people oblivious to one another's lives intersect at this terminal with its frenzied and all too familiar vistas caught in an unrelenting loop of noise and chaos, the paths, the stories, and even perhaps the destinies of the arriving passengers dispersing throughout Istanbul, and of those carried away from Istanbul almost trade places. Between arrivals and departures, dreams, hopes, adventures, lives are scattered across the city, across the country. It's as though destiny stands in wait at the crossroads, spinning its webs.

Once the bus begins moving, after the last farewell, the woman recoils in her seat restlessly, as if sitting on a bed of nails. To allay a bit of her anxiety, Zozan tries to strike up a conversation, 'Where are you traveling, auntie?' she begins. 'Are you going to Tunceli, too?' 'No... I will get off at Elazığ.' 'The non-stop busses were all full, except for the ones leaving much later. We are in a hurry, so picked the first bus we could find.' As she speaks, her eyes begin to well up, her words get knotted in her mouth. Her voice, tremulous, elegiac, suggests that the source of her hurry, whatever it may be, is a deep, raw sadness. It is clear that she can barely contain herself; as if she is afraid of coming unglued, she must think that her only safeguard is to sit absolutely still, like a hardened mass. Zozan realizes that she shouldn't force her, and withdraws.

A little later, the woman manages to ask, almost with a calm voice, 'Will you let me know when we arrive? I am familiar with neither roads nor signs. I'm afraid to miss Elazığ.' 'Don't you worry, auntie,' Zozan replies, 'even if you fall asleep, I'll wake you up.' 'I don't think I'd sleep tonight,' the woman says.

Zozan had hoped for a much more pleasant trip at least this time; the sad presence of this mournful woman sitting next to her weighs down her spirit, rends her heart. She is seized with the feeling that her life, heretofore overshadowed by a sorrow that followed every joy, was warning her against too much happiness, letting her know that from here onward, too, it would unfold according to its unalterable rules.

She thinks of all the busses on the road at this moment, all their passengers being carried to different cities, to different lives. As night descends, who knows how many of the passengers in those busses stare sleeplessly at the road, how many of them rest their heads against the glass and doze off, how many of them dream, how many of those dreams portend good news, how many bad? Those going back home for a visit, those reassigned to new posts, merchants traveling from city to city, inspectors, those on national service, the newlyweds on their way to kiss the hands of their elders, vacationers, those who leave their father's hearth to chase their luck in big cities, those who couldn't gain a foothold in big cities and return, those exiled from one place to another, retirees in search of a quiet life, divorcees sent back to their family, those sent off to military service, those returning, those running away from something, those chasing someone, the madcap whose eager spirit runs ahead, anxious to reach his destination, the dying who, after long years, wish to visit their birthplace for one last time, suitors on their way to ask for their beloved's hand, runaways, fugitives weary of the checkpoints, those on leave, those returning, those simply traveling, for the sake of traveling... While counting one by one and adding up in her head the paths, the passengers, every conceivable destiny bifurcating along the road, Zozan slowly falls asleep without even noticing.

As the Istanbul-Tunceli bus travels through mountains and valleys, clouds, trees, streams, vistas, cities zoom across the window and disappear in the back until the next ones.

Translated from the Turkish by Aron Aji

Aborted City

HATICE MERYEM

Tearaways unite –
make this city cheap,
solitary, quiet, and livable.
Got kids? Get neutered!

On one of the steep streets up in Dolapdere, where rubbish stands about like fringe décor, above the door of one of the old houses that seem to lean on each other so as not to collapse, this was written in white chalk.

If the wrenching in my loins hadn't forced me to perch on the threshold of the house directly opposite, there was no way, given the state I was in, that I would have seen either the door or the writing above it. Now with my hands pressed hard against my stomach, I murmur in delirium:

'Not my hand, oh hand of our Mother Fatima[6], take this pain, cast it away, away beyond Mount Kaf[7]! Not my hand, oh hand of our Mother Fatima, take this pain, cast it away, away beyond Mount Kaf! Not my hand, oh hand of our Mother Fatima, take this pain, cast it away, away beyond Mount Kaf!'

With all my might I struggle to keep control of my body,

6. Mother Fatima, daughter of the Prophet Mohammed and wife of the Prophet Ali; the paragon of benevolence, goodness, perfection and fidelity. She is believed to have healing abilities that can be invoked by reciting this lamentation.
7. Mount Kaf is an insurmountable mythical mountain, often mentioned in Turkish fairytales.

my will, to stay conscious. Drops of sweat the size of rosary beads stream from my temples down to my neck. My mind is a mess. My befuddled brain sends a sweet sensation of numbness to my feet and hands and then, after restoring some life to my numb feet, takes me by my weary hands, leading me in, out, in, out, in to the gardens of childhood, and together we wander. My befuddled brain and I are in a garden adorned with chrysanthemums, snapdragons, four o'clocks, and lilies, where the sun nests and cats litter kittens in every corner. In that same distant, solitary place, there is this old woman who recites over and over her comforting refrain, and the red bricks that she heats as she tries to soothe the relentless pain in my knotted stomach[8]. I am certain that my childhood still exists, out there somewhere. Somewhere, where all childhoods live hand-in-hand, like sisters and brothers. In one of them, in mine, an old woman is constantly heating bricks for a little girl... An old woman keeps on heating bricks for a scrawny little dark-skinned girl... An old woman is constantly heating bricks... For a motherless girl, a scrawny little dark-skinned girl...

'Almighty Allah, oh help us His Prophet and Messenger!' With this cry ends one of the secret rites of childhood.

That painful place inside of me is relieved, a bit, I believe, by the old woman's healing prayer. I'm exhausted, terribly. Slowly I lift my lolling head, now grown too large to bear, from my chest and my gaze falls upon the writing above the door opposite me, and I read it once again.

Tearaways unite –
make this city cheap,
solitary, quiet, and livable.
Got kids? Get neutered!

---

8. Heating bricks and pressing them against a woman's stomach is a traditional Anatolian method of soothing period pains.

118

Could all the tearaways really unite one day?

And what about those with kids – should they really get neutered?

According to a renowned international city planner, 'In twenty years' time, all those yuppity, supra-urban 'Winsome Homes' and 'Fare Well Cities' they're so eagerly erecting are going to screw us for good!'

Apparently, the children who grow up in these gated communities – built supposedly to take the weight off the city's shoulders and offer escape from the city racket, and so intricately designed to provide every imaginable luxury, from playgrounds to cinemas, from shopping centres to primary schools, from car parks to swimming pools – would end up 'racist'! Each community would have its own religion, language, flag, and, with time, traditions. What's more, these children would become such enemies of society that they would voraciously attack vehicles on the motorway and rip them to pieces. They would even start their own gangs and wage war against kids from other communities. And when that day comes, the old folks would call these unfortunate kids tearaways.

Perhaps the hour of revenge for all my poorly tended woes had arrived; on the prowl, they had come out from hiding to ensnare me in my moment of weakness. Here on Earth, on this threshold, freezing my arse off, in a state of agony, with these ridiculous thoughts barging through my head, two little girls, barefooted, in raggedy clothes, their hair in greasy clumps, appeared at the top of the slope. They headed downhill, swaying their skirts along the way. Oblivious to my existence, either they didn't see me, or they didn't care. One of them swiftly slipped an object pressed tightly in her palm into the hand of the other. Then, without saying a word, they ran their separate ways. I saw their faces, for a brief moment. I was shocked at how the faces of these two mini people could appear so old, so storied.

Only art, and the streets – with a fist to the jowl, a knee

to the groin, a swinging uppercut, a punch in the eye, knocking you out before you know it – give the human face its final touch. With the dark shadows and eerily purple bags beneath their eyes, these girls' faces were like living records, the proof that they'd been dealt a heftier share of the streets than of art. In a constant dogfight with the skin of life, they wore their scratches boastfully, like battle scars. While the faces of those leading quiet lives gently 'settle' over forty-fifty years, theirs were forever in a state of punishment, standing on one leg in the corner. Each of the girls' faces seemed to me like one big dirty look. One of them quickly passed by, pounding her way up the slope.

At that moment, I thought again of the international city planner's prediction. Now I better understood just who the city would belong to once the prim and proper ladies and gentlemen moved out, to the gated communities with their swimming pools. Suddenly, all the pieces of the great conspiracy fell into place; it was crystal clear to me now. The key to the 'Plan to Take Over the City', a grand hoax that wouldn't have occurred to me in a thousand years, was concealed there in the sentence above that door. I grew excited. They say excitement is good for pain; my cramps went away just like that.

The children who sold tissues under the pitying eyes of the Big City People, women selling sweet scented lavender on street corners, the miserable looking, manly-faced thirteen-fourteen-year-old boys, sniffing paint thinner and smoking cigarettes and sleeping in parks and ATM booths, the shoeshiners, the Gypsy flower girls, the lunatics, the tearaways... All of a sudden I understood that every single one of them was actually an ironclad soldier serving this 'great purpose'. I was overtaken by a great sense of exhilaration. I was now dead certain that the exchange I had witnessed a moment ago was part of the conspiracy to further the 'great purpose', and that the girls had given each other a password, a secret code.

Well duh, who gives more thought to a dying animal

than the parasites that feed off it? You can hardly blame them. If the international city planner and the prim and proper ladies and gentlemen weren't going to worry about making this city cheap, solitary, quiet and livable, of course somebody else would have to take care of it. Besides, weren't these people, once confined to the slums, now loitering in packs around the big hotels in the heart of the city? They'd become so pervasive that not a day went by when the newspapers and TV didn't speak of them; they'd even become fodder for 'shocking' news specials.

How on earth hadn't the Big City People thought of this before!

Wandering throughout the city as silent and invisible as ghosts, they had become so artful as to render us ignorant to their existence. They were nothing but an organism that had infested every corner of the city. An organism, because in their declarations they didn't say 'I', they said 'we': 'we street children', 'we beggars', 'we, we, we…', always 'we'. That's right, with their filthy hands, slovenly appearances, and their sometimes timid sometimes brazen attitudes, they were like a halo that we wore on our heads unwittingly. That's why, when we look up, we see nothing but the filthy sky.

I got up. I looked up the hill. The sun was perched at the summit. My pain had receded, together with the girl climbing up towards the sun, which was just a hundred metres away, her twiggy legs visible beneath her skirt. I set after her. 'I've seen your plan, make me part of the 'great team' serving the 'great purpose.' I want to change this city, too, just like you do,' is what I wanted to say to the poor little girl. But the thing about people with kids getting neutered sent a violent spasm to my loins, as the contractions grew even more painful, nearly splitting my body in two.

The girl turned into one of the streets perpendicular to the slope. I picked up my pace, ignoring the pain in my loins, and when I reached the entrance of the street, I saw her lying there on the pavement, curled up asleep on a large, dusty piece of cardboard. Me being the trickster I was (like all Big City People, I suppose), I figured that, noticing she was being followed, she must have been faking it. And if I were to tell her what I was thinking, she would sit up, suddenly, like a cat leaping to its own defence – hunched back, bared teeth, hissing, on guard – and say:

'Who the hell do you think you are? It's because of smart-arse morons like you that this city's the way it is. *What*? Make *you* part of the team? What the hell are you talking about? You people have got bad blood, now sod off!'

I was sure that's what she would say.

Yet all these half-baked, conflicting thoughts only added up to yet another of the nightmares we pathetic Big City People had to confront each and every day.

When I got a bit closer to the poor little girl lying there on the ground, I saw, in the light of the sun shining on her face, that her chest was gently rising and falling. What peace and unity? What great purpose? What great team? What big city? The poor little thing was sound asleep. These pretty little misfit creatures don't possess an ounce of the sick ideas that have seeped into the heads of us Big City People, I thought to myself.

This time the pain hit me in the back, like a twist of the knife. I pounded my way uphill, my knees to my nose. When I got to Harbiye, my only hope – and Allah be praised, hope never runs out – was to reach my two-room flat in Beşiktaş. I was broke, and I didn't even have the strength to cross the street. I was barely able to drag myself across, with the effort of a diver who's expended his last bit of oxygen just a few metres from the surface. I was drenched in cold sweat. A few benevolent people looked at me as if to ask whether I needed help.

I crouched next to the bust of Uğur Mumcu, hopeless. The sesame ring seller standing there next to the newsagent looked at me with eyes full of kindness.

'Would you like a sesame ring?' he asked.

I shook my head no. I was dying of thirst. I motioned for him to come over. He walked up to me.

I asked him to buy me a box of juice. But he couldn't hear me, because he was just standing there, stiff as a rod. I motioned again, 'closer' I told him, 'closer'. This time he almost put his ear in my mouth.

I asked him again: 'Could you get me a box of juice?'

He walked over to the refreshment stall a few steps away and soon returned with a box of juice. This time he leaned forward gently and placed the box in my hand. I couldn't help but feel a sense of gratitude towards him. I say I 'couldn't help' it, because gratitude is one of the strongest of emotions, but it's also equally fleeting, and so I'm reluctant to expend this fickle feeling on just anyone – at least, not under normal circumstances. The sesame ring seller returned to his stand. He kept an eye on me, though as if trying to be careful not to intrude.

I thought of all those benevolent people. The pretty ladies whose eyes fill with tears at the thought of helping street children, their doorkeepers, and their doorkeeper's children, and the well-learned gents who give glue sniffer boys money to buy their dope. It's not that I'm cruel or stern by nature or anything, it's just that I can't take benevolent people. When helping others, they look like they're concealing a crime that no one knows about, like they're trying to cover it up. Maybe that's why I can't stand them. Besides, benevolent people would bet you anything that they couldn't even hurt a fly. Well, who could? I mean, a human being hurting a fly! A human being couldn't hurt a fly if he wanted to; at the most, he'd just kill it.

I stood up, staggering, and the fruit juice I'd just had went swish swash in my empty stomach. The Uğur Mumcu bust seemed to have three heads. I knew I was the one with the problem – it wasn't like the great Uğur Mumcu was gonna go sprouting a few extra heads!

I dragged my exhausted feet towards squeaky clean

Nişantaşı. I walked past the shiny windows of a string of shops like Gianna Versace, Armani, Burberry's, Lina's Sandwich, foreigners *en masse*. Smiley faced djinns were prancing all around, pumping air into my skull; they were so hard-working, they just wouldn't stop. At one point, I felt a few drops of warm liquid running down my leg. Imagining all the terrible things that could happen to me out on the street, I felt my stomach rise. I paused in front of a shop that sold just vitamins, which, when not suffering from excruciating contractions, I would gaze upon in awe. I leaned against the wall and went through my pockets, but only came up with a bit of change. I wanted to jump into a taxi and tell the driver, 'Take me as far as this change will get me.' I was suddenly afraid of being raped and murdered. Strange, huh? Considering the state I was in!

I began tottering my way down from Teşvikiye. The drops streaming down my legs were forming a trail behind me. Probably because I was retching and gagging by now, I felt as if my gullet just popped out my mouth, wrenching my entire stomach out with it. Doing my best not to bite my gullet, I grabbed my stomach just in time to keep it from falling out and splattering onto the ground.

I barged into the courtyard of Teşvikiye Mosque, postal address Rumeli Avenue No: 150. By the look of the size and quality of the crowd, it seemed yet another person of distinction had died. Funerals here are always for people of distinction; the tiny neighborhood mosques are more than enough for the funerals of the indistinct masses. The courtyard was packed with other people of distinction, come to pay their final respects. I virtually rolled down the stairs to the toilet. I tried to pull the door open but it was locked. Sealed tight, no way in. You know how they say that God grants mortals a final chance before death? Well, at that moment, the toilet warden suddenly appeared behind me.

'Here's the key, sister.'

What a good, what a blessed man the deceased was. It

must have been for his sake that the toilet warden noticed me. I locked the door as soon as I got in. I sat down on the *ala turqa* squat toilet. I leaned back against the cold tiles and waited, my eyes fixed upon the piece of paper which was decorated with cheap, plastic red roses. It read: 'Leave it the way you want to find it.' 'I want to find it clean, really clean, really really clean,' I whispered in a barely audible voice. The toilet monster reached out from the toilet hole. It latched on, ripping out what it wanted from my uterus. The womb spat it out, the toilet hole swallowed it up.

I could hear the hodja's voice coming from the courtyard: 'In his lifetime, this good man... El-faatiha.'

The toilet warden was pushing against the door and calling out, 'You okay, sister? Say something. What the...'

And then... And then life calmed me down. My hair damp with sweat, I too joined the congregation and said one helluva *fatiha* for the soul of the deceased. I left the mosque courtyard and went to a nearby café for a warm cup of tea. A woman sitting on the pavement, perched next to the wall of the mosque courtyard, asked me for money, motioning towards the babe in her arms and using Allah as her middleman. I searched my pockets again, but only came up with a few coins. As I dropped them onto the handkerchief spread out before the woman, I looked at the babe, flies buzzing around its face. For a moment, my eyes met the insulting, pitying gaze in the baby's beady eyes. It didn't even try to disguise the two treacherous, sarcastic, cynical curved lines on the sides of its mouth. This innocent babe's face was exactly like the faces of the girls I saw up in Dolapdere – one big dirty look. I quickly turned my eyes away from this dark and depressing scene and towards the branches of an oak tree.

I picked up the pieces of my shattered face. I straightened my eyebrows, wiped the sides of my mouth, and pulled my cheeks up. By the time I got to the café, I felt happily refreshed. I fluttered into the café, light as a bird. I asked for a cup of tea and then I wrote the bastard's name on a cigarette and inhaled it slowly. I was just about to walk out when the waiter called out after me.

'Sister, you haven't paid for the tea!'

I motioned for him to come over.

'I just had a miscarriage at the toilet in Teşvikiye Mosque, and I'm exhausted,' I said, quietly. The waiter looked at me with shocked and unbelieving eyes.

'Just kidding,' I said, cheekily. 'I don't have any change. Is it okay if I pay later?'

'Oh, okay, no problem then, that's okay'.

As I walked out the door, I heard him tell another waiter: 'You know that woman who just left? She must be crazy or something. She says she just had a miscarriage in the mosque toilet.'

Outside, the breeze sent a shiver through my bones. At that moment, the mosque, the breeze on my face, the coolness of my wet hair on my neck, my weightless body, the warm bitter taste of strong tea on my tongue, life, it all seemed so incredibly important to me. At that moment, like a chemical formula: It doesn't do you any good to give birth to another. And with every minus we multiply.

Translated from the Turkish by
İdil Aydoğan and Amy Spangler

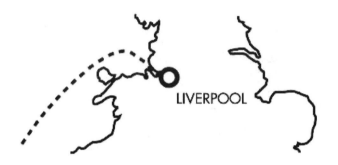

LIVERPOOL

Bread, Circuses and Replica Shirts

ALEXEI SAYLE

Angel suspected that if it hadn't been for his injury he wouldn't now be feeling this disturbing sense of dislocation. To be alone in an alien city with so much time on his hands could only lead to unhealthy introspection. It had not been what he expected. He had been signed from FC Malaga to Liverpool for a substantial transfer fee, there had been a photo-call, handshakes all round with the owners, but then on his first day of training he'd fallen awkwardly and hurt his back, an inconvenience which meant he would not be able to play for the team for at least a month. This in turn meant that rather than working out with the other players, he had to come into the club for long periods of physiotherapy. He didn't particularly mind the time he spent being pulled and stretched and poked, but it did mean he hadn't been able to get to know his fellow professionals at all. Angel had had one conversation with the manager in which he'd been told that as soon as he was well, great things were expected of him, but after that he'd been abandoned.

Since then his routine had been long, lonely hours by himself, exercising in the club gym or undergoing therapy sessions with the medical staff, and then long evenings spent alone in his smart modern hotel on the waterfront. The hotel's staff didn't help with his feelings of disassociation either; he found them to be like big, amiable animals: delighted to see you, but as soon as they turned their backs, you disappeared totally from their consciousness. He would order a coffee at breakfast from a waitress and then thirty minutes later, still without coffee, the same woman would drift past, see him as if for the first time and say in the friendliest manner possible, 'Hello love, you look all lost, can I get you a coffee?'

Angel had always hoped he would play in England one day. Obviously the Premier League was the most competitive and lucrative league in the world, but he had a particular affection for Britain. The village from which he came, in the foothills of the Sierra Nevadas, had always had a number of British living in it. When he was young there had only been a handful of pioneers, but in the last few year their numbers had grown until they made up perhaps five or ten percent of the population.

He was a sensitive and thoughtful boy and there had always been something about him which set him a little apart from his own people: he found the rough peasant ways of his fellow Andalusians – their superstitions, their crude jokes and their earthy passions – faintly repulsive. Even his skill at football was unusual in a village where basketball was the favoured game.

As he grew older, he found himself slowly drifting towards the little group of foreigners who lived in the centre of the village. First he hung out with the British kids and through them he eventually became adopted by the entire expatriate community.

The more he got to know the British, the more he found to admire in them. Many of those who lived permanently in the village or who owned holiday homes were writers, filmmakers or artists, and even the ones who were builders or plumbers possessed an originality of thought, a love of culture, a wit and a quickness of mind that he felt no Spaniard could ever match. Angel was determined that one day he would play football and live in their country, the country of Dickens, Rushdie and Helen Fielding, Constable and Tracey Emin, Pugin and Wren, Norman Foster and

Richard Rogers, Jeff Beck and Johnny Vegas.

Even when he went to play for FC Malaga his biggest fans were foreigners: the club had over two thousand foreign season ticket holders; most of them were British and he was their hero. So when Liverpool FC finally came calling he didn't give it a second thought before he signed to play for them.

Unfortunately, because of his injury, his time in England so far had not been what he'd expected. The time up to the accident was a blur and in the long empty days afterwards he had started to experience this unsettling sense of dislocation. In the many hours when he had nothing to do he would drive his modest Toyota to some part of the city and walk around. The physios had said gentle strolling would help his back.

However, on these walks, there were a couple of matters that disturbed him. When he had been in Spain the only thing he ever found unsettling about the British was the way they drank alcohol, throwing it down with a demented concentration so at odds with the relaxed tipsiness of his own people. In the centre of Liverpool, particularly on the weekends, the amount of aggressive drunkenness he saw amongst young people, especially women, went far beyond what he had seen back home, and made him feel extremely uncomfortable. He wondered if Sir Salman or Richard Dawkins or Jeanette Winterson got shitfaced on a Saturday and then threw up in a litterbin.

The other thing was the amount of terrible urban decay he saw almost everywhere. He knew from his drives that there were fine parks and expensive houses and fancy shopping malls, but when he drove from his hotel to the stadium or from the motorway into the centre, all he seemed to see were dilapidated shops, empty patches of land, burned-out pubs and boarded-up houses. And the dereliction seemed particularly bad around the stadium – a couple of times he had walked around the perimeter of ground, and what he saw there fascinated and appalled him. Leading away from the brick walls of the football ground on three sides were rows and rows of abandoned and boarded-up houses. Angel couldn't understand how the British people he so admired could let a part of one of their greatest cities fall into such a terrible state. But then he thought that perhaps the British people around the football ground were of a type he hadn't encountered before. At first he'd wondered if there was a big hospital nearby, so ill and listless did many of the people seem who he saw wandering along the litter-strewn streets and between the mean shops and dilapidated pubs.

None of the other players, as far as he could tell, had any opinion about the ruined area in which their stadium, with its opulence and glamour, seemed to have landed like an alien spaceship from a much richer planet. His team mates would arrive at the club in their giant 4x4s, or if it was match day, on the team coach, and paid no heed to the rows and rows of houses with their blank windows blocked up by metal shutters with which he was becoming obsessed.

One day there was a gap of two hours between physiotherapy sessions, but rather than going to lunch, he slid along the corridors that permanently smelled of liniment and, feeling as if he was playing truant from school, passed between the gates and stood for a moment on the street. Then Angel crossed the road and headed into the abandoned neighbourhood opposite; soon the noise of the rattling buses and the jabber of the excited tourists had faded and around him all was silence.

Occasionally in the distance he would glimpse a bent figure shuffling along, appearing and disappearing between the rows of boarded-up houses, or he would see them crossing the patches of cleared land where long grasses and wild flowers nodded in the breeze as if they were Alpine meadows that had travelled from their mountain homeland so they too could gaze in awe on the mighty football stadium. Generally though, the streets were deserted.

Looking more closely at the houses, Angel's confusion

grew. As far as he could tell these were perfectly sound dwellings, much better in fact than those he had seen people living in in other parts of town – their only problem was that they had huge slabs of metal bolted over their doors and windows. He took out his mobile phone and began taking pictures of these sad-eyed dwellings.

On the edge of his hearing Angel heard a high-pitched buzzing, as if a mosquito was attacking him; it was only when he looked up that he saw two boys, on scooters, helmetless, approaching fast from the north. They rode right up to him, taking up station on either side so that, with his back to the wall, his exit was blocked. Both were about fifteen years old, heads shaved and skin the same unhealthy, old newspaper colour as the others he had seen drifting around the neighbourhood. Since he'd come to Liverpool, Angel had grown used to people looking at him with interest. The doctors and physios were aware that he was a valuable asset and already there were many in the town who had seen his picture in the paper and knew of his prodigious talent. It had been a long time since such cold and uninterested eyes had surveyed him as if he was nothing at all. Letting the engines of their scooters subside to an angry grumbling, one of the boys said:

'What do you think you're doing here mate?'

Though he was discomfited by their stares Angel was not particularly afraid, he knew if it came to a fight he was stronger and fitter than both of them, but then he thought *What if they have guns?* and he was a little more concerned.

'Who told you you could take pictures?' the other asked. 'You with the bizzies?'

'You some sort of grass?'

Angel did not know how he would have answered if a voice hadn't said from over his shoulder.

'Hey, leave him alone.'

He turned and saw that one of the houses behind him hadn't been abandoned as he'd thought. The door was open and a man stood on the step. He was perhaps in his mid-forties, though his face was lined and cracked as if he'd borrowed his grandfather's skin. His hair was grey and cut close to the head and a ring of stubble encircled his chin. A shabby colourless T-shirt hung from his stringy body, greasy and stained black tracksuit bottoms encased his legs, while on his naked white feet were tartan slippers people generally only wore when they were in a hospice.

The two boys slowly altered the direction of their shotgun gaze until they too were looking at the man.

'Whot?' the first boy asked, slightly animated for the first time.

'I said leave him alone.'

'What's it got to do with you, Grandad?'

'Nothing much, but don't you recognize him?'

'No.'

'Well, you're bothering Liverpool's latest signing. The new Spanish teenage maestro.'

'So what?' said the first boy, unmoved. 'We're blues, we hate the reds.'

'Yeah,' replied the older man, 'but isn't your boss a mad keen red? I don't believe he would take kindly to you harming their best new player.'

'How do you know who our boss is and what he likes?' the second one asked, unable to keep the curiosity out of his voice, the child that he still was suddenly peeking out from his round, pasty face.

'Me and your boss we were at school together... for a while we were best mates.'

'You... and our boss were friends?' the first boy asked, looking at the man on the doorstep with obvious contempt. 'What happened?'

'Well,' the man said smiling to himself, 'I made the mistake of passing all me exams...'

For a second the first boy paused, then said, 'Maybe we'll harm the two of yiz, then nobody'll find out about it.'

'Naw,' said the man, a smile again playing across his face. 'See, one of the sad things about kids like you is you spend your whole time calculating who you can harm, who you have to suck up to, what you can get away with. We both know you can't get away with that, not here, not today. So what's going to happen now is I'm going to invite this young man into my house and you are going to go away and do your thing elsewhere. Angel,' he said turning to the young Spaniard, 'would you like to come in for a cup of tea?'

'Yes thank you,' Angel said, speaking for the first time. After a moment he eased past the man and into the dark interior of the little house.

The homeowner closed the door behind them, then they stood in silence for a second until they heard the petulant buzzing of the scooters fading away.

'Thank you for that,' Angel said.

'Oh you're welcome son. My name's Tony by the way, I know what you're called.' And they shook hands. Angel looked around him. The street door opened straight into the front room, which at some point had been knocked through so now it ran all the way to the back wall, which had a single grimy window overlooking the backyard. The whole space seemed to be lined with books crammed and jammed onto rough wooden shelves. There was no sight of the walls – as far as Angel could tell they might not exist and the house was only held up with books.

In the corner there was a battered armchair and resting on the seat cushion a thick Penguin classic and a pair of cheap, plastic reading glasses.

Tony swept these off and said to Angel, 'Sit down son, sit down, I'll make us that cup of tea.'

While the man clattered about in the kitchen they conducted a shouted conversation.

'Once again, thank you for getting me out of that situation,' Angel called.

'Oh, you can look after yourself – you're a fit young man,

135

healthy and sleek on good food and exercise and admiration. I was just as concerned for those boys, they've been raised on a diet of Cheesy Wotsits since they were six months old. Their bones are probably as brittle as Twiglets.'

'They might have had guns.'

'Yes, there is that...'

'So are you a Liverpool fan?'

Tony shouted back, 'No, I'm afraid I'm not a fan of, of that place opposite.'

At this point he returned with two battered mugs of tea, one of which he gave to Angel, then pulled over a tired looking kitchen chair and sat facing the boy.

'Can I ask you why you were taking photos of these tinned-up houses?'

'Well... it seemed sort of odd...'

'Such dereliction and poverty so close to that place where footballers earn a hundred thousand pounds a week and a replica shirt sells for forty pounds... which is about what I have to live on for seven days?'

'I suppose so, yes.'

'Do you know who's responsible?'

'No.'

'Your employers. In the 90's, the club thought they were going to expand the stadium so they started buying up houses all around the ground, on the quiet, and they've got hundreds now, all boarded-up and falling apart. Then their plans changed. Now the scheme is they're going to take a huge slice of our local park instead; but this area has been bighted for well over ten years, and of course the council is supine, lets them do whatever they want. You can imagine what all this had done for house prices. The old people, who bought their own houses, they live in fear and yet they're stuck: they'll not get another mortgage and, if they're forced to sell, they'll end up in sheltered housing.

When there was still a few more people living round here, a deputation went to see one of the Liverpool FC executives about the state of the area. And they asked him, 'Don't you care about your community?' And he replied, 'Our community is the world.' What he was saying was those of us who live in the shadow of that thing don't matter, it was the TV audience that mattered, the business community that mattered, the supporters that mattered, not us.'

Angel felt uncomfortable being in such an odd, oppressive room with such sudden intensity. He sipped the tea, which was terrible, and thought the milk might be off. 'Oh that is a shame,' he said.

'Yes, it is a shame,' Tony replied. Pulling his chair closer and staring into Angel's eyes, he suddenly asked, 'You ever heard of Juvenal, son?'

'The Brazilian who plays in goal for Real Sociedad?'

'No,' he laughed, 'the Juvenal I'm talking about was a Roman poet who lived nearly two thousand years ago. He felt, I suppose as a lot of old fellers feel, that the society he lived in had fallen from its once lofty ideals and was now a decadent, wretched thing, dedicated only to feasting and fleshy entertainments. Juvenal felt the people of Rome, once so noble, had sold their birthright to any leader who would sate their squalid pleasures. He wrote a poem about it which he called 'Satire X'.'

Then, staring at the ceiling in a quite disturbing way, Tony began to recite:

'Already long ago, from when we sold our vote,
the People have abdicated our duties;
for the People who once upon a time
handed out military command, high civil office, legions
    — everything, now
restrains itself and anxiously hopes for just two things:
bread and circuses.'

He paused for a second. 'Bread and circuses, does that sound familiar to you, son? What would that be now. Pot Noodles and football, eh? Because football is definitely our circuses, one of the ways in which they control us.' By now Tony's voice had risen and there were little flecks of foam at the corner of his mouth. '…Football, X Factor, Amy Winehouse, they fill our minds with stuff that doesn't matter so we don't think about any of the things that do matter, like how come News International never pay any tax? Why is it wrong when Russia invades countries, but alright when we do it? Why do I live in a street of tinned-up houses?' Tony paused and visibly seemed to collect himself. 'I'm sorry son,' he said to Angel, who'd been looking at the older man with an expression of concern on his face. 'I get a bit carried away sometimes.'

'That's OK,' the boy replied. 'I mean it's sort of interesting, nobody has ever spoken to me about football like this, I had always thought of it as something that only brought pleasure to people.'

'Of course, of course,' Tony said. 'You have a sublime talent and you only wish to express it.'

'Yes. Yes, I just want to play football.'

'Of course. Why should you care that football has become completely detached from its neighbourhoods, from its roots, and is now a plaything for gangsters, Arab sheiks and Asian Kleptocrats?'

'Err… yes.'

'Yes, you close your eyes. And of course the fans, with their demented addiction to their clubs, they don't care. They'd do anything, accept anything. If they heard Darth Vader and the Galactic Empire had bought their team they'd just say, 'Great, now we can buy that left-sided midfielder we've been missing'.'

'Hmmm well I…'

'Of course, you know it will end quite soon for you, don't you? You'll play your football and you'll come to love it so much, then one day the boss whom you thought cared about you and was your friend will come to you and say, 'Angel, we don't need you anymore and we're selling you to

Stockport County.' But you'll have had three good years, it doesn't necessarily mean your life is over.'

Angel rose, spilling a little of the rank tea onto his trousers. 'I think I have to go back to the ground now, Tony.'

Tony appeared again to collect himself. 'Oh dear. I've been going on again haven't I?'

'No, no it was interesting.'

'I'm sorry, I was ranting.'

'No, it's fine.'

'I'll show you out.'

'Thank you.'

Tony opened the door for the young man and he slowly stepped, blinking, into the spring sunlight.

'Maybe I'll see you again,' Angel said.

'No you won't,' Tony replied.

'No, I suppose not.' And he walked off in the direction of the stadium, his head bowed in thought.

The next day, Tony was walking back from the corner shop twirling the tiniest plastic bottle of milk it was possible to buy round and round his finger, when he heard at his back the two boys approaching. One steered his machine along the pavement behind him, the other rode alongside in the road. Tony did not look at them but stared ahead, a strange little smile playing across his face. The one in the road said:

'We told our boss about what happened yesterday.'

'Telling the truth that's always good,' Tony said, still not looking at them.

'You were right. He said if we'd messed with that Spanish feller and he'd found out about it, he would have stapled our heads to the wall with a nail gun.'

'Glad to be able to offer some useful advice.'

'But what he couldn't understand was why you helped the Spanish feller. He said years ago you'd gone nuts and after you'd come out of the place where they put you, you'd become the most demented blues fan that he'd ever met.'

139

Tony stopped, and turning to the young men asked, 'Boys, do you know what the essence of talent is? It's confidence, and confidence is perhaps just a quarter of a percent of a person's ability. Millions of boys like you possess the physical attributes to play in the Premiership, but what they don't have is that blind belief in themselves. The ones who succeed never consider that they might fail, or get injured, or that what they're doing is evil or pointless. But it's a fragile thing, and yesterday I took away that Spanish boy's confidence. When he gets over his injury he'll play a few games, but I reckon he'll never be the footballer they thought they were buying; they'll just sell him back to wherever he came from, if he's lucky. I've just cost the reds twenty million pounds.'

'Yeah, sure you have,' the first boy said. 'And how did you do that?'

'I pointed out to him that modern football is a force for oppressing the masses, that it has become a soulless and deracinated toy for criminals, dictators and torturers and when his talent declines they'll toss him aside like a used yoghurt pot.'

'And he believed it?'

'No, he didn't believe it, not completely. If he'd been your average player he wouldn't have heard what I was saying at all – his curiosity and his intelligence were his undoing. There isn't another one who would have walked around here taking pictures. What I did was, I planted a tiny seed of doubt in his mind and that'll be enough to chip away at that quarter percent of his confidence.'

'But you think it's all crap right, what you said?'

'No, no, I think it's all true, I just want Liverpool to fail and for Everton to play a bigger part in it, that's all.'

Authors

Liverpool's **Dinesh Allirajah** was a founder member of the North West writing group 'Asian Voices, Asian Lives'. A well-respected jazz-poet and workshop leader, he has performed at venues all over Europe. His short story collection *A Manner of Speaking* is published by Spike Books, and his stories have been widely anthologised (notably in *The Book of Liverpool*, Comma Press, 2008).

Artur Becker, son of Polish-German parents, was born in 1968 in Bartoszyce (Masuria/Poland). He came to Germany in 1985 and lives in Verden an der Aller near Bremen. Becker is a novelist, poet and essayist. His publications include *Der Dadajsee* (Lake Dada, novel, 1997), *Dame mit dem Hermelin* (Lady with Ermine, poems, 2000), *Die Milchstraße* (The Milky Way, stories, 2002), *Kino Muza* (Cinema Muza, novel, 2003), *Die Zeit der Stinte* (Time of the Smelts, novella, 2006), *Das Herz von Chopin* (Chopin's Heart, novel, 2006) and *Wodka und Messer. Lied vom Ertrinken* (Vodka and Knives. Song of Drowning, novel). His poetry collection *Ein Kiosk mit elf Millionen Nächten* will be published in 2009. Becker has received numerous awards and literary scholarships. Among others the Autorenförderung des Literaturfonds Darmstadt and writing residencies in Krakow, New York, and Olevano. His complete work so far is to be awarded with the Adelbert-von-Chamisso-Preis in 2009.

Dr Franco Bianchini is Professor of Cultural Policy and Planning, at Leeds Metropolitan University. He was Research Fellow at the Centre for Urban Studies, University of Liverpool (1988-1992), and previously Reader in Cultural Planning and Policy at De Montfort University in Leicester. His publications include *Cultural Policy and Urban Regeneration: The West European Experience* (with M. Parkinson, Manchester University Press, 1993), *The Creative City* (with C. Landry, Demos, 1995), *Culture and Neighbourhoods: A Comparative Report* (with L. Ghilardi Santacatterina, Council of Europe Press, 1997) *Planning for the Intercultural City* (with J. Bloomfield, Comedia, 2004) and *Urban Mindscapes of Europe* (co-edited with Godela Weiss-Sussex, Amsterdam, Rodopi, 2006). He has acted as advisor and researcher for organisations including Arts Council England, the UK government's DCMS, the Council of Europe and the European Commission. He was appointed by the President of the European Parliament to the selection panel responsible for designating Cork as the European Capital of Culture for 2005. In 2007 he was part of the group of experts chosen by the Slovenian government to select Slovenia's choice for the 2012 European Capital of Culture. Since 2003 Franco has collaborated with the Liverpool Culture Company in developing 'Cities on the Edge'.

Dr Jude Bloomfield is an independent researcher and writer on urban cultures, planning and citizenship, a translator and poet. She specialises in intercultural planning and urban imaginaries. Recent publications include *Planning for the Intercultural City,* (with F. Bianchini, Comedia, 2004) and 'Researching the Urban Imaginary: resisting the erasure of places in Weiss-Sussex' in *Urban Mindscapes of Europe* (Weiss-Sussex G. and F. Bianchini eds, Rodopi, 2007). A book based on life histories and narratives, *Intercultural Innovators: Learning from Life Stories* (Comedia), is in preparation. She is currently collaborator, in the artists' group – We Sell Boxes We Buy

Gold – on interventions in the Olympic zone of east London. Her long poem, 'Reclamations', drawing on walks, narratives and memories of the Lower Lea Valley was performed in Hackney Museum in December 2007 and will be published in 2009.

Marseilles-born author **Christian Garcin** has published a wide range of novels, short story collections, poetry collections and criticism. His five novels are *Le vol du pigeon voyageur* (éditions Gallimard, 2000) – winner of the Prix du Rotary International – *Sortilège* (éditions Champ Vallon, 2001), *Du bruit dans les arbres* (éditions Gallimard, 2001), *L'embarquement* (éditions Gallimard, 2003), and *La jubilation des hasards* (éditions Gallimard 2005). He's also an academic and translator into the French, most notably of the works of Jorge Luis Borges.

Jim Hinks (ed) is a graduate of The University of Manchester's MA in Novel Writing, where he was a recipient of the Curtis Brown First Novel Award and the Jerwood/Arvon Scholarship. He's taught creating writing at The University of Leeds and is the editor of *Brace: A New Generation in Short Fiction* (Comma, 2008).

Gdansk novelist and short story writer **Paweł Huelle** spent his early writing career as an employee of the Solidarity Movement's press office in the late 1980s. He subsequently achieved enormous success (both domestically and in translation) as a writer, and has been honoured with many prestigious awards. His first novel *Weiser Dawidek* (1987) – described by critics in Poland as 'the book of the decade', 'a masterpiece' and 'a literary triumph' and eliciting comparisons to Günter Grass and Bruno Schulz – has been widely translated. Huelle followed *Weiser Dawidek* with *Moving House and Other Stories* (1991), *First Love and Other Stories* (1996), *Mercedes Benz* (2001), and *Castorpe* (2004). The latter novel was published in English translation (Serpent's Tale, 2007) and was shortlisted for the 2008 Independent Foreign Fiction Prize.

Adam Kamiński was born in Poland in 1978 and is a poet, writer, playwright, and literary critic. His first collection of poetry, *Stąd, czyli z Raju,* was published in 2000, followed by his first collection of stories, the acclaimed *Sam* (Alone), published in 2006 by Gdansk University Press. Several of his plays have been broadcast on Polish national radio, and he was recently shortlisted for the 'Golden Pen of Sopot Award'. His latest collection of stories, *Kapłanka* is published in 2008.

Jean-Claude Izzo shot to international fame in the 1990's as the author of the now legendary 'Marseilles Trilogy' of thrillers (*Total Chaos, Chourmo* and *Solea,* published in English translation by Arcadia Books). His distinctive brand of vivid, pacy crime writing has captured the imaginations of readers the world over, encapsulating Marseilles' simmering issues of race, politics, organized crime and big business, and igniting a whole genre of 'Marseille Noir.' Before his death in 2001, Izzo also earned a reputation as a formidable short story writer with the collection *Vivre Fatigue.*

Peppe Lanzetta was born in Naples in 1956. He first worked as a lyricist with singers Edoardo Bennato, Pino Daniele, James Senese and Franco Battiato. His theatrical debut was *Neapolitan Repented* (1983) which was followed by *Roipnol* (1984), *The Gospel according to Lanzetta* (1986), *Lenny* (1988), *Dear Achille, I am Writing You* (1990) *The Worst of Lanzetta (*1993), *Tropic of Naples* (1998), and 'Give us Back Our Dreams' (2001). An actor, screenwriter, and the director of short films, he has worked with Piscicelli, Tornatore, Cavani, De Crescenzo, Loy, Martone, Asia Argento, and Scimeca. His published works include *Burn up my Life* (Baldini & Castoldi, 1996), *A Love with Expiration Date* (Baldini & Castoldi, 1998), and *A Trip to Naples* (Paravia, 1997), *Children of a Lesser Bronx* (Feltrinelli, 1993), *A Neapolitan Mexico* (Feltrinelli, 1994), *A*

Post-Dated Life (Feltrinelli, 1998), *Tropic of Naples* (Feltrinelli, 2000) and *Give us Back Our Dreams: Ballads* (Feltrinelli, 2002).

Hatice Meryem is an Istanbul based novelist and short story writer, and former editor of the literary magazines Okuz and Hayvan. Her books include the novel *Kısım Kısım Yer Damar Damar* (İletişim Yayınları 2008), and the short story collections *Sinek Kadar Kocam Olsun Başımda Bulunsun* (İletişim Yayınları 2008) and *Siftah* (Varlık Yayınları 2000), from which her story 'Aborted City' appears.

Murathan Mungan is known in Turkey as the author of poetry, plays, short stories, novels, screenplays and songs. His first collection of poems, *Osmanlıya Dair Hikayat* (Stories about Ottomans) was published in 1980, making Mungan an overnight success. His output remained prolific, and various poetry books followed, notably *Yaz Gecer* (Summer Passes) and *Metal*. He has written four stage plays, which earned him wider success. *Mahmud ile Yezida*, and *Taziye* are two of the most staged plays of the modern Turkish theatre, and his screenplay *Dağınık Yatak* (Messy Bed) was later filmed by director Atif Yilmaz in 1986 starring the Turkish actress Müjde Ar. His short stories have been anthologised in numerous volumes such as *Kirk Oda* (Forty Rooms) and *Paranin Cinleri* (Genies of Money). Mungan is also regarded as an icon of the Turkish gay movement.

Valeria Parrella was born in 1974 and lives in Naples, where she trained as a specialist in Italian Sign Language. Following the publication of her debut short story collection, *Mosca più balena* (Mosquito and Whale, Minimum Fax, 2003) she became widely regarded as one of Italy's most exciting young authors, and is winner of Renato Fucini Prize 2005, and the Zerilli-Marimò Prize 2006 for Italian Fiction in the US. Her other books include *Per grazia ricevuta* (For Grace Received,

Minimum Fax, 2005), *Il verdetto* (The Verdict, Bompiani, 2007) and *Lo spazio bianco* (The White Space, Einaudi, 2008).

Liverpool-born author **Alexei Sayle** is a comedian (with numerous TV appearances to his credit, including The Young Ones and Comic Strip in the 80s and Alexei Sayle's Stuff in the 90s), novelist and a short story writer. His debut short story collection *Barcelona Plates* was published to widespread acclaim in 2000, and was followed by *The Dog Catcher* (2001), and novels *Overtaken* (2003) and *Weeping Women's Hotel* (2006), all published by Sceptre. In 2007 he revisited the Liverpool haunts of his youth to film the 3-part BBC documentary *Alexei Sayle's Liverpool* (BBC 2008). His latest novel, *Mister Roberts*, is published by Sceptre in 2008.

Translators

Aron Aji is a dean at St. Ambrose University, Davenport, Iowa, USA. A native of Turkey, he has translated fiction, poetry and plays by Turkish writers into English. His translation of Bilge Karasu's *The Garden of Departed Cats* (New Directions) won the 2004 National Translation Award. Aji also received a 2006 National Endowment for the Arts fellowship for his current translation project, another novel by Karasu, *The Evening of a Very Long Day*.

İdil Aydoğan works as an instructor at the Department of English Language and Literature, Ege University, Izmir, Turkey. Hatice Meryem's 'Aborted City' is her first published translation in English.

Rebecca Braun (nee Beard) gained a BA in French and German at St Edmund Hall, Oxford, and a D.Phil in German literature at New College, Oxford. She is the translator of Damaris Kofmehl's Shannon (London: Hodder & Staughton, 2002), and has also gained considerable experience translating art criticism for the Viennese gallery dreizehnzwei. She currently holds a Leverhulme Early Career Fellowship at the University of Liverpool, where she teaches and researches on authors and the media in Germany from 1960 to the present. Her most recent publication is the monograph *Constructing Authorship in the Work of Günter Grass* (Oxford: OUP, 2008).

Helen Constantine taught languages in schools until 2000, when she became a full-time translator. She has published two volumes of translated stories, *Paris Tales* and *French Tales*, and is currently editing a series of '*City Tales*' for Oxford University Press. She has translated *Mademoiselle de Maupin* by Théophile Gautier and *Dangerous Liaisons* by Choderlos de Laclos for Penguin. She is married to the writer David Constantine and with him edits the international magazine *Modern Poetry in Translation*.

Antonia Lloyd-Jones is a translator of Polish literature. She has translated five books by Pawel Huelle, three of which, including *Castorp* and *Mercedes-Benz*, have been shortlisted for the Independent Foreign Fiction Award. Her other translations of fiction include *The Birch Grove and Other Stories* by Jaroslaw Iwaszkiewicz (now being adapted for the London stage) and *House of Night, House of Day* by Olga Tokarczuk. She also translates non-fiction, and her latest publication is *Like Eating a Stone* by Wojciech Tochman, about the aftermath of war in Bosnia. Her translations of Polish poetry have appeared in periodicals including *The Edinburgh Review*.

Helen Robertson is a Paris-based translator specialising in literary, cultural and film translations from French and Italian into English. Her previous work has included screenplays, shorts stories, extracts from novels, film pitches and synopses. She translates on a daily basis for the European film website www.cineuropa.org and as a volunteer for Amnesty International France.

C.D. Rose lived in Naples for fifteen years, where he learned to speak Italian, and some Neapolitan. He has translated writings on art history, experimental cinema, philosophy, archaeology, microbiology and the sewer system around Caserta. He has published a number of short stories, including

'Violins and Pianos are Horses' in *Parenthesis* (Comma).

Amy Spangler is the translator of Aslı Erdogan's novel, *The City in Crimson Cloak* (Soft Skull, 2007) and co-editor and co-translator (with Mustafa Ziyalan) of *Istanbul Noir* (Akashic Books, 2008). Co-owner of AnatoliaLit Copyright and Literary Agency, Spangler is currently an instructor in Translation Studies at Okan University and a guest instructor in the same at Bosphorus University. She resides in Istanbul.

Special Thanks

The editor and publisher would like to thank the following people for their advice and support throughout the project: Sir Bob Scott, Andrew Farquhar, Jackie Malcolm, Myriam Tahir, Fiona Doorey, Rachel Myall, Maura Kennedy, Francisco Malheiro, Jim Friel, Anna Carolina Brauckmann, Rebecca Morrison, Ewa Ayton, Anna Battista, Mirjana Cibulka, Tim Parks, Ina Studenroth, Sophie Moreau, Barbaros Altug, Serra Cili, and the staff of The Festival of the European Short Story (Zagreb, Croatia).

Decapolis
Tales from Ten Cities
ED. MARIA CROSSAN
ISBN 9781905583034

Featuring: Larissa Boehning (Berlin), David Constantine (Manchester), Arnon Grunberg (Amsterdam), Emil Hakl (Prague), Amanda Michalopoulou (Athens), Empar Moliner (Barcelona), Aldo Nove (Milan), Jacques Réda (Paris), Dalibor Šimpraga (Zagreb), and Ágúst Borgþór Sverrisson (Reykjavik).

'The European short story is clearly in vigorous form.'
– Matthew Sweet, *Nightwaves, Radio 3*

Madinah
Citry Stories from the Middle East
ED. JOUMANA HADDAD
ISBN: 978 1905583201

Featuring: Nedim Gursel (Istanbul), Gamal Al-Ghitani (Alexandria), Fadwa Al-Qasem (Dubai), Ala Hlehel (Akka), Hassan Blasim (Baghdad), Yousef Al-Mohaimeed (Riyadh), Elias Farkouh (Amman), Nabil Sulayman (Lattakia), Joumana Haddad (Beirut), and Yitzhak Laor (Tel Aviv).

Elsewhere
Stories from Small Town Europe
ED. MARIA CROSSAN
ISBN: 978 1905583133

Featuring: Gyrdir Eliasson (Iceland), Frode Grytten (Norway), Micheal O Conghaile (Ireland), Danielle Picard (France), Mehmet Zaman Saclioglu (Turkey), Ingo Schulze (Germany), Roman Simic (Croatia), Jean Sprackland (England), Olga Tokarczuk (Poland), and Mirja Unge (Sweden).